# THE CHRONICLES OF
# MARÍA TERESA DE VILLALOBOS

## SAN JUAN BAUTISTA DE PUERTO RICO, 1650

LORETTA PHELPS DE CÓRDOVA

---

# THE CHRONICLES OF
# MARÍA TERESA DE VILLALOBOS

## SAN JUAN BAUTISTA DE PUERTO RICO, 1650

### A NOVEL

SAN JUAN

Design by Leamir Candamo Pou
Drawings by Gabriela Pérez
Production by Jay Chevako

*For my family and for my beloved Puerto Rico*

*San Juan, Puerto Rico*
*1650*


*You, dear reader, are almost surely my descendant. For my hope is that this diary will stay within our family for years to come. Thus, you may know from whence you spring. Perhaps you may learn from my joys and sorrows.*

*At my advanced age, I now look forward to the next life, in the company of Christ, the Virgin and all the saints, and my family and friends who have gone before. Someday you and I may meet there as well. Resisting spiritual doubts and beating off despair, my faith still endures, shaky and anxious as it may be at times...*

*I have loved this life on earth. My long, thick black hair has whitened in my eighty-six years. And my once-slim figure has withered to a stick. Yet eyes can still see and hand is steady. As I set my quill to paper, the past arises in my memory as though it were yesterday...Annotating my old writings brings back those years so vividly...*

*Last week, among the yellowing papers in the exquisitely tooled gold-inlaid chest, carved by the mozárabes in Córdoba and carted by Mother across the ocean, are segments of my diary written on and off throughout my long life. These days I prepare for death. But I look at the words I wrote and remember the girl who sought beauty, love, excitement and adventure, in sum, that explosive combination of idealistic dreams and energetic self-interest that equals youth. I have passed through the prudence and caution of middle age. Looking towards eternity has freed me from temporal concerns. Renewed is a carefree spirit*

*I've not known since childhood. I read these lines written so long ago and smile in remembrance.*

## Chapter One

❦

I was born aboard ship on October 26 of 1564, a precipitous act. My mother had planned on bringing me into this world in her new home of Puerto Rico, where Father had accepted a position as the official and only physician-surgeon. His friends in Salamanca thought him mad. Who else would want to settle on that deceptively lovely, green isle? Since Juan Ponce de León had conquered the Taíno Indians half a century ago, little of import had happened there. But the settlement did need a physician. There mysterious fevers and sores unknown in Spain felled dozens, and hurricanes, torrential rains and plagues of ants and mosquitoes could make daily life a torment.

No more gold was to be found in the rivers. Indians were few. Most of the surviving Taínos had escaped to the southern islands of the Caribs. With few to work the cane fields or small sugar mills, or tend the yucca fields and fruit trees, agriculture languished. Some people actually went hungry on this verdant isle. Landowners could not afford new black slaves, so Portuguese traders bypassed the island.

Even Spaniards were in short supply. Those who could fled to our new possessions in the West for gold, silver and glory. The riches of Potosí and New Spain (México) lured the ambitious. The misnamed "Puerto Rico" was ignored. Only soldiers, priests, and government employees like my father would live here willingly – at least for a while. To stop the run of able-bodied workers, one governor threatened the branding iron or amputation of a hand to those who would escape without a permit. Yet the rallying cry continued: "God take me to Perú!"

Oddly, it was in this tropical prison house that my father would seek his fortune. The Crown had promised him prosperity and standing. Doctor Diego Cataño, licensed physician of the great university of Salamanca, would receive so much land and salary in addition to a high position that surely our large family might flourish there. He wanted my mother to share his dreams.

Many others had gone off alone to this New World and not returned to wife and children in Spain. Warfare, malaria, and mysterious disease had killed many a strong warrior. And the lure for power of life and death over poor Indians intrigued lecher and wastrel to disappear forever from civilized Spain. This New World offered so many dreams and pitfalls to so many frail men.

So, my father would do things differently. Overcoming a natural prudence and chronic pessimism, he signed the lucrative contract as medical officer for the military garrison of this remote Spanish watering station. Perhaps the commitment would serve as a stepping stone for México or Perú, should Puerto Rico fail him.

\*\*\*

My family told me of my birth and the crossing, since I was hardly in condition to observe the surroundings. The ship was named Catalina, for the poorly treated Queen of England, princess of Aragon, Henry Tudor's wife. Though she was put aside by Henry VIII, the daughter of Isabel and Fernando had a resilience and courage that made her a splendid model for a seagoing vessel.

This sturdy barque had left Cádiz and then set sail for the Indies from Ferro in the Canary Islands. Twenty-nine people shipped aboard: Doña Mercedes de Bazán de Cataño, eight months pregnant with me. Her husband Diego, the physician. Their daughter and three sons. The Catalán captain, three officers, ten crew, two indentured servants from Extremadura, three young Yoruba female slaves from Africa chosen for the Governor's residence in Puerto Rico, and a Dominican chaplain from Valladolid. Plus, two Basque Jesuits bound for the Philippine Islands, and four Andalusian soldiers destined for El Morro Fort in San Juan.

It was sunrise, two and a half weeks out at sea. My sister, fifteen-year-old María del Pilar loved this moment best of all. Most people still slept, so solitude and space reigned. Before long, all sixty-eight feet and fifty-five tons of ship would be throbbing with life.

Her brothers would be teasing her about having a romantic fixation on the ship's pilot, while she'd try to ignore the brats and help her queasy mother. Pilar had decided to make the best of her father's folly, keeping her eye open for a good husband who might take her to México or back to Spain. Though the Cataños and her mother's family had little money, and only tenuous connections at court, her lineage was old enough to tempt an ambitious parvenu or a solid honest official. Large grey eyes and ash brown hair set off a long oval face that many found attractive. Her appearance was elegant and austere. She was a full woman, ready for marriage and her own life.

She could not but resent Father's taking her off, at this crucial age, to nowhere. In Puerto Rico they'd be surrounded by rough soldiers and peasants. Few families would equal their social position. Truly, almost anywhere else in Spain's vast empire would have been better.

Perhaps María del Pilar would have to join the convent, a refuge for women who would not marry a distasteful or inadequate suitor.

Now only the dawn watch crew was awake. The men were busy hauling up seawater to spill on the oaken floor, then scrubbing it down with stiff straw brooms. By the end of the three-week voyage, brooms would be limp and frayed. The morose-faced chief boatswain silently stood by.

Meanwhile, Pablo the ship's lad intently watched the sand clock. He and every boy in Spain remembered that Admiral Columbus had complained about the ship's lad who'd fallen asleep and lost the time on that first discovery voyage to America. What an inglorious way to make history! The youngsters were official timekeepers. They spelled a four-hour watch, marking each half hour by the turn of the fragile Venetian glass.

There was just enough sand to last thirty minutes.

Day's blue brightness gently nudged aside the pale dawn. Deep indigo sea emerged from night-black waters. The vast ocean, marvelously still, put on its morning face as stars fled the sky.

Still brushing sleep from his eye, the lad cleared his throat, reedy voice preparing to greet the day quavering the traditional chant. Singing in a minor key, a bit off-tune but with great vigor, he intoned: "Blessed be the light of day And the Holy Cross, we pray!"

It was an effective alarm. Soon everyone came tramping onto the deck. When all were assembled, the chaplain led them in the Pater Noster and the Ave María, other prayers in Latin mixed with Spanish in the common holy argot. The ocean was calm that day, so the priest set up the makeshift altar to say Mass. Otherwise he would recite prayers but not risk consecrating the host and wine in a rough sea.

After Mass, the ship's lad put out watered wine and hard biscuits for breakfast. The gentry had brought along their own candied fruit, though not much was left after two weeks. As Pilar silently munched a fig and watched the scene, she picked another fruit for her mother. She considered the leather-faced captain attractive. But almost surely married. Besides, who would want a seafarer as a husband? At least at the beginning, she wanted a man next to her.

There were only two cabins. The captain occupied one, the Cataño family the other. Everyone else slept in the big hold below, in hammocks like those invented by the Taíno Indians. Cooking was as primitive as the facilities. Such Ávila delicacies as roasted lamb and sesame cake needed good, thick stone ovens.

But on board the ship's deck was a mere sandbox protected by a hood. In heavy weather there was no cooking at all. The usual diet was salted fish, cheese, pickled beef and pork, biscuits, wine, rice, beans, nuts, sugar, garlic and dried fruits. Since the Crown was enticing my father to settle in that notoriously poor island, the Catalina's provisions were better than on many sea voyages. The family all agreed the food wasn't too bad. That is, everyone but my mother, who could hardly eat for seasickness. It was all she could do to keep down coconut water laced with a little rum, brought from the Canaries.

The Catalina was earth brown, trimmed with red. Crosses and heraldic devices adorned the sails. Below the water line, pitch-covered wood repelled barnacles. The Catalina was sturdy and seaworthy, specially designed for enduring these long ocean crossings.

My oldest brother Francisco Javier loved the voyage. He told me about the sails bellying in a sweet balmy wind, lines creaking with strain. How the bow plunged through the foam. Flying fish and *dorado* and dolphin often swam alongside. The constant roll annoyed only those with delicate stomachs, like my mother, Doña Mercedes de Bazán de Cataño. She, of course, had reason. Me.

Francisco Javier was named for Ignacio de Loyola's brave follower from Navarra, who died on an island off China. My brother found this first voyage so thrilling that he later put to sea as ship's officer, travelling to our Philippines across the Pacific and even to the ports of Cathay. Francisco Javier said sailing was like being Adam in Eden, free, wild, limitless. Who could settle for boring dry stable earth after this?

The smell of daybreak drying on the wooden deck, the feel of salt spray on the cheek, the thwacking sound of line against the mast, the rhythmic heaving of the caravel…

My mother could. She hated the sea. Like most well brought-up women of Ávila, she knew how to read her prayers in Spanish and Latin, embroider on silk, play the lute, ride a horse, manage a kitchen and servants, attend to her husband's business. But she certainly wasn't prepared for the rolling of the ship as she awaited childbirth.

The day of October 26, labor pains began, a whole month ahead of time. They would last for several hours. Doña Mercedes called for my sister and Esperanza, her indentured servant from Extremadura. The girl was an orphan who had lived in a midwife's house, so she knew something of that art, making her invaluable to our family. The chaplain stood at the door, waiting to administer Baptism to me and, if things went badly, even the Holy Oils to my mother.

Silently Pilar sat down and held her mother's hand, looking around the crowded cabin rather than at Mother's agonized face.

Doctor Cataño's books overflowed two boxes: medical tomes from the age of the Greeks, especially Aristotle and Galen, and then from the Spanish Moors. Religious readings such as the favorite *The Imitation of Christ*. Chivalrous romances *Amadís de Gaula* and *Tirant lo Blanc*. The histories of Pérez de Guzmán, Plutarch, Chacón and de Escabías. Philosophies of Augustine, Gregory, Boethius, Cicero and Córdoba's own Seneca. Doña Mercedes's personal favorite was Dante's *Divine Comedy*, which fused poetry, history and philosophy.

On the back wall of the jam-packed cabin, straw-filled pallets piled one on the other, to be lowered at nightfall for the whole family,

A sour odor persisted in the cabin, in spite of Juana's quickness to mop up whenever Doña Mercedes vomited. The servant threw crushed cloves to clear the air. They heard the ship's boy burst into song again with the traditional refrain:

"To our God let us pray
To give us a good voyage
And through the Blessed Mother,
Our advocate on high,
Protect us from the waterspout
And send no tempests nigh."

Doña Mercedes smiled to hear Pablo's young voice and crossed herself, as she geared up for labor. Her face was pale, though each day she'd walked a few steps to catch the sun and smell the fresh salt air. Body might be frail, but her character was tough.

Her spirit was bolstered by what they'd seen three nights past. A sudden storm had risen. Clouds had hidden the full moon.

Thunder echoed on the vast sea and roiling waves battered the ship. Suddenly a crackling, moving ball of light danced at the mast head. The rare and beautiful sight, called "Saint Erasmus's fire" or "Saint Elmo's", is a sign of God's favor. With its appearance, Doña Mercedes knew the ship would survive the tempest and the child in the womb would not die. She'd already lost three babies at birth, and prayed fiercely this one would live.

Then straightaway the storm had calmed. Remote stars returned to the vast black heavens, giving a glimpse of eternity. The sturdy small ship thrust through the still-uncharted sea, the dark glistening waters reflecting the mystery above. Doña Mercedes had dreamed about the strange world that lay ahead. But that was three days ago.

Now was time for bringing another life to the world. Outside the cabin, her husband tried to concentrate on his chess game with the chaplain and not think on his wife's suffering. Esperanza would know what to do.

Each child's birth is but a repeat of what has happened countless times on this earth. Yet only we live our lives, which are to us special and unique. We do not merely emulate what our ancestors did. Our struggle, our soul, is particular. After six hard hours of bothering my mother, of threatening to enter this world and to begin my journey through life, I finally emerged. A month ahead of schedule, I squalled at leaving the comfortable dark womb of absolute certainty. Mother was strong and determined and loving, so we both survived.

I was ugly, as most babies are. They baptized me María Teresa, after the Virgin and my mother's childhood friend and distant cousin from Ávila. They claim names help shape a child's character. And though my own life has been far from that of my namesake, her deeds have haunted me.

Though so much different from the sainted model, I have always had her as a constant underthought in my life, a sort of compass to provide direction in perilous moments. Her strong character gave me strength.

Mother had the good fortune of early knowing María Teresa de Jesús. The patronym shows her family's Jewish tradition, since many converts to the Church had adopted names of Christ and the saints. My mother and she lived close by in that windy chilly hilltop walled city. Though a couple of years older, Mother often played with Teresa and her cousin.

"She was intelligent and holy and full of life even then, a sweet and vibrant friend," Mother recalls. "More than anything, though, she was intense and joyful. About everything." And she told us about the incident mentioned in "Mi vida", the book María Teresa wrote about her life. Teresa and her boy cousin packed a few clothes for the trip and went off down the road, on the way to Jerusalem to convert the Mussulman. Mother knew about it but was pledged to secrecy. She was too cowardly to join the young pilgrims in their mission, so had never even been considered as a cohort. About eight years old at the time, the two young adventurers had not gone far when discovered missing. They were quickly found and brought back home.

By the time Mother married Father, Teresa was already battling with her soul and had entered the Carmelites. And by the time I came to the world, Teresa had surmounted a long period of paralysis and debilitating pain. Even more telling for her, she had emerged from constant doubt and ennui, galvanized to pray with such intensity she became a mystic, to act with such intensity she reformed the very concept of religious life in Spain and throughout Christendom.

When we consider how dangerous the Inquisition can be to a woman visionary, and even more so to one of Jewish lineage, her great influence is even more remarkable. In spite of her fame, she has remained translucent in her dedication to truth, love, simplicity. The "interior castle" she wrote about – the God-dwelling soul – was made of glass. Clear.

Yet her wry approach to everyday life and the need to shun self-importance were authentic. Her comments went to the grain.

About a woman *beata* who had suffered persecution, Teresa said, "She and two other souls that I have seen in this life...who were saints in their own opinion, caused me more fear...than all the sinners I have seen."

Teresa's view of the Christian in the world has been my bulwark in so many ways. While our society prizes honor and rank of the individual above all, she combats social status to place virtue and friendship with God and human above all. While others stew about what is acceptable, she rejects prejudice.

And within Spain, she has drawn many new Christians, *conversos,* as benefactors and followers. Their numbers are great, as most surnames with reference to saints or Christ reflect *converso* origin. We know that *limpieza de sangre* or purity of blood (meaning a "true" Christian, not a Jew or Muslim heretic pretending to be one) is an obsession with our people. The insecurity prompted by the fact that any malevolent witness could ruin a family and lead to death has prompted all sorts of deceptions. But anxiety of recrimination for her Jewish background has never moved Teresa. She has been fearless in attacking hypocrisy with astute wit and even amusement. And she herself has admitted doubt within her fierce search for God. A brave woman.

Later on, her follower, the great poet and mystic Juan de la Cruz, would define the time of spiritual agony as a time most mystics and even more common folk endure: The Dark Night of the Soul. Who has not known a barrenness of spirit, a sense of futility? How often does not the abyss consume one's will? Through all my life and in the midst of prayer, I have pondered my own existence and sought its meaning. Now, ready at any moment for the tomb, I still ponder and hope...And fear...

Knowing I was named for this extraordinary person, and Mother's friend to boot, makes me treasure the person and path that is Teresa de Ávila. I aspire to follow that path, though with much less passion than she. I would not even wish to have her courage. It would be too earth-shattering. But each of us is a solitary pilgrim, wandering through life. Our reality is a continual search...

Father, a good man though a chronic doomsayer, later claimed that my early birth was the first bad omen.

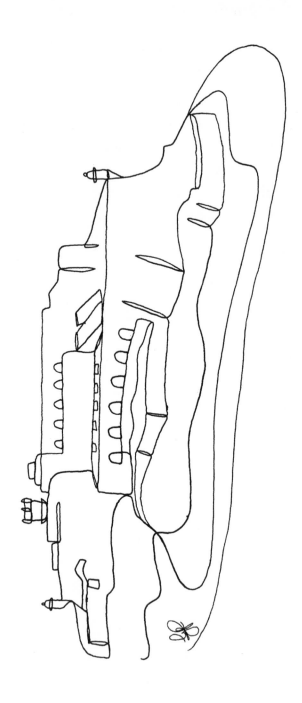

*Chapter Two*

~ • ~

A week later, we made port at the palm-fringed deep harbor of Puerto Rico, San Juan Bautista. Reflecting the golden sand floor, the bay's blue water glittered in the bold bright sun. At the horizon rises the cordillera, stark and jagged against the vivid bright sky, the color of Our Lady's mantle.

As we sailed by the rocky headland, the crew spotted the gallant flag of Spain waving from the fortress and fell to shouting huzzahs.

The cliff line abruptly dropped. It levels out to a narrow sandy spit where dinghies beach. At harbor mouth's opposite side, an earth-hugging, seagrape-littered islet jutted out from the mainland. And whitecapped reefs, extending well into the harbor mouth, chop the cay's surrounding water. This means the only passage to the bay lies directly under the formidable cliffs.

In those days, we were just beginning to build the fortress called San Felipe del Morro. A round stone and mortar tower perched atop the point, on the barest foundation of today's massive walls. This was the governor's residence, grandly called Palacio de Santa Catalina and La Fortaleza.

The governor-general himself came down to greet the ship. Of course, the population numbered but a few hundred and our arrival was an exciting event for everyone – from high to low degree. The ship put in as close as possible, and tenders took passengers and crew through the calm water.

After proper bowing and presentation of documents, the officials led our family to the house provided by the Crown. It was close by the governor's house, La Fortaleza.

A soldier-guard led the way.

An oxen cart carried all our worldly possessions through the gate and up the dusty street, past the cathedral to this lovely spot. Mother knew she would likely never return to Spain. She had brought all her treasures – Portuguese linen, *Catalán* ceramic dishes, iron cooking tools and pots, a box of fine *mozárabe* tiles from *Andalucía*, several decanters of Venetian blown glass, three fine silk dresses, two carved ivory fans and swathes of cotton fabric to make dresses. She'd also brought nine seedlings of the best stock of grapefruit, orange and lime trees from Valencia. Between her belongings and Father's books, the oxcart overflowed.

This place is still our home, though we now have another rustic house in the country in the area called

Bayamón. In San Juan the narrow two-story building enters right off the dusty street. Two massive studded doors creak open to an ante-room and the interior patio. Three windows on the second floor share a long balcony to look over the street. Cool stone floors, high ceilings and thick masonry walls protect the dwellers from the enervating tropical heat. This type of building reflects the first settlers' Andalusian roots. It could have been a house in Córdoba or Écija.

The only drawback is the flat roof. For the arid south of Spain that's fine. But here rains beat daily in furious, short showers. Roofs become water collectors with constant leaks, even while the underground cistern stores most of the runoff.

Overwhelming all else is the view. The sapphire blue bay lies below, its color a legend from ancestral tales. We look across the water's wide expanse to mangrove forest and sandy shores, where a thousand birds seek out the clams and oysters at muddy low tide. Beyond the bottom area extend grassy plains and streams.

Rising above all is the cloud-shrouded mountain range where the Taínos' gods lived long before the white man came. As I write this now, I look out my window to see that same glorious sight. Truly, it calms my soul. The memory of this vista has refreshed me all through my turbulent life.

Our family, then, installed itself with relative comfort in what would become our true home, far from the mother-fatherland.

17

***

The Admiral had written King Fernando and Queen Isabel about his discovery of Puerto Rico in 1493, saying: "...I found another island of which I saw only the north coast as drawn, about the same size as Sicily, of more land and beauty than I'd seen to that date, to which I gave the name of San Juan Bautista.... It has many good ports and much water and big rivers, with highlands and lowlands, with big trees and all worked and planted for ages, singularly well maintained. Here I saw very good houses with adornments, and in the streets, cane fences and nets that went from the settlement to the sea. On one side and another was a path to the sea, where at the beach was a kind of roofed dock area, so well built it would have been acceptable in Valencia."

The Admiral exaggerated. The Taínos lived in simple cane huts.

***

The capital then, when we arrived, was a mere village with a small but solid fort, churches and convents, official houses and buildings, several dozen residences, hospital, taverns and a licensed brothel. I was told the Bishop received tithings from the brothel, though I never dared ask him directly. Shame. All told there were four or five streets in those days, with perhaps a hundred-fifty buildings, about half the size of what it is now.

In trying to bring Spain to the New World, the city now has all the traditional elements. The cathedral commands the top of the hill, facing the city gate and making it the first glimpse one has on entering. Facing the cathedral, immediately to the right of the gate winds the hilly approach to La Fortaleza. Back of the cathedral is the Plaza de Armas, where the militia drills and bullfights take place. Facing the plaza is the *cabildo*, where municipal civil government business is conducted. The home of Juan Ponce de León's family perches higher yet on a hill, looking over the bay to the mountains. He never lived in it, since he was seeking the fountain of youth.

\*\*\*

I quote from the work of Gonzalo Fernández de Oviedo, which he wrote in 1535. He said about Puerto Rico's conquistador and first governor:

"There was a fable about a fountain that could rejuvenate old men: this was the year 1512. So many Indians talked about it, that Captain Johan Ponce de León and his people...seeking it sailed around the islands of Bimini, for more than six months. It was a big joke among the Indians that the Christians would waste so much time looking for this fabulous fountain. The Indians talked about it to disturb old men...Declining sexual power, waning physical strength and disappearing youthful good looks all bothered the conquistador...who lacked sense and self-discipline.

He let his vanity lead him to believe this nonsense...In truth, he had earlier been an honorable and noble person..."

\*\*\*

Yet, with all the hopes to imitate the wealth and grace that was Sevilla, San Juan was a poor, humble town. No doubt. The delicious soft air carried pernicious disease, though the site was far better than the bug-infested Caparra which Governor Juan Ponce de León had chosen first. Here in the new town the breezes kept away the insects. But it was a place of paradox, of the unexpected. Perhaps that it is why I always will love this city.

Our *hacienda* had still to be built on the land assigned to Father. It was across the bay on an immensely fertile fluvial plain. There he dreamed to build a *cortijo* worthy of Andalucía. But, contrary to promises made, he soon discovered there were few workers and no slaves. The rich land tract was overrun with wild guava trees and poisonous yucca and unruly vines and tall sawgrass. A few cattle and many goats and pigs ran wild. To work the land would depend on the governor's good will whether indentured servants or black slaves and Indians would be available. And if Father could find a very good *mayordomo* to run the place.

Father quickly learned that he and the governor-general were not cut from the same cloth. On returning home from the first meeting, he feared the worst. Seldom do good soldiers make good governors.

But no one could deny the governor's military prowess. Named Don Francisco Bahamón de Lugo, he was veteran of cavalry campaigns in Flanders and a tough, competent soldier.

When just appointed to the post, Bahamón quickly showed his mettle for war. He could scowl like a pirate, baring his teeth ferociously and frightening his subordinates. His tone of voice was harsh, and the volume loud. He could also daunt the enemy.

Fortunately, Father's job was to cure rather than to fight, and he dealt with the governor-general on a different plane. He brandished scalpel and needle rather than cutlass. Though he visited the Palacio de Santa Catalina daily to treat Don Francisco's chronic indigestion, perhaps due to over-eating, most of his work was done next door. The little hospital held perhaps thirty beds. Its terrace looked straight over the harbor view, a natural stimulant for those recuperating in the hammocks. Father had brought all his medical instruments and books with him. That was well, for they were the only ones on the island.

# Chapter Three

In January of 1565, soon after our own arrival, Bahamón was hunting wild pigs in the highlands of Coamo when news arrived of a ferocious attack on the west coast settlement on the banks of the river Guadianilla. A band of ferocious Carib Indians had swept in from the sea in their giant wooden canoes. They sacked the village, killing three men and taking thirty captives, most of them women. Then the war party headed east in their formidable war boats, following the coast. These Indians were the terror of the Caribbean, strong, fearless and known as man-eaters. The word "cannibal" is a corruption of the word "caribe". The women prisoners would surely end either as slaves or food. Dozens of warriors, both men and women, easily rowed hundreds of leagues in their fast dugout canoes, coming up to Puerto Rico and Santo Domingo from their safeholds in Santa Cruz and San Martín.

When Bahamón heard the news of the raid, he immediately gathered a makeshift force of mounted settlers and slaves from the Coamo area. My brother, Francisco Javier, just 13, tall and healthy, had been part of the hunting party, so he became part of the expedition. The improvised army rode pell-mell for the island's southeast coast, some armed only with farm tools. Once there, they hid near the mouth of the Guayama River, protected by the still waters and dense, gnarly vegetation of the mangroves. They waited.

They could hear the Caribs talking and laughing as they paddled their long boats upriver to take on water for their long sea voyage. Their next stop would likely be Vieques, on the way to Santa Cruz and south.

The Indians and their captives pulled ashore where the fresh water entered the estuary. As they climbed out of the canoes, dragging the women with them for sport, the Indians were surprised by the Spaniards, who burst out of the mangroves. The Indians fell back. Even so they were fierce fighters and it must have been a bloody horror. Most of the Indians were killed, though one canoe escaped. The reports said simply, "Sixty-seven Indians died and many Spaniards." All the captives were rescued and returned to their homes.

Unfortunately, Bahamón's splendid fighting ability and bellicose spirit left little room for administrative talent. He soon alienated the very people he was sent to govern, a regrettable pattern often seen in the heavy-handedness of Spain in America. In spite of lessons learned in such magnificent plays as Lope de Vega's *Fuenteovejuna*, reality here was often the contrary. Pleading to the crown – after first appearing at the *Audiencia* in Santo Domingo – meant going to Sevilla. It was costly and time consuming. America spawned many venal rulers, who made mockery of church and crown.

\*\*\*

In that much loved and performed play, the villagers of Fuente Ovejuna rushed as one to kill the commandant who had raped their women and tortured their men, crying: "Long live Fuente Ovejuna! Now we see the tyrant and his accomplices. Fuente Ovejuna, and the tyrants die! Viva King Fernando! Let the bad Christians and traitors die! Our true lords are the Catholic Monarchs."

*(¡Viva Fuente Ovejuna! Ya el tirano y los cómplices miramos. ¡Fuente Ovejuna, y los tiranos mueran! ¡Viva el rey Fernando! ¡Mueran malos cristianos y traidores! Nuestros señores son los Reyes Católicos.)*

Not only did the villagers act as one in executing the tyrant, but they bound together when questioned and tortured by the authorities to learn who was responsible. All answered "Fuente Ovejuna!" At the end of the play, Fernando and Isabel pardon them for their actions, since there'd been no other recourse for the villagers. Of course, that was on stage – not real life. Even so, the play shows that deepset conviction we Spaniards hold – that tyrants must not be tolerated by decent people. That sense of personal judgment is also echoed in the Catalonian oath of allegiance to Fernando, which begins: "We swear loyalty to you, who are no better than we..." Even so, to put that idea into action requires courage that is often lacking...

\*\*\*

Father soon learned the awful reality that faced us. His salary, which had seemed generous when quoted in Spain, was in fact a pittance here. It took 360 *cunos* of gold in Puerto Rico to equal 100 *cunos* in Spain. The economic imbalance stifled trade. Few boats even set anchor in Puerto Rico. The boats that did arrive would usually be at some remote cove. Clandestine trade on the coast went on, since tax could be avoided. The few sugar mills were in ruins. Puerto Rico could not compete with the abundant riches of México and Perú. As years passed, the island eventually became totally dependent on them. In 1586, a huge annual stipend of Mexican silver was assigned annually to pay government and church expenses in Puerto Rico.

This lifeblood, called the *situado,* was often swept away by pirates or hurricane.

So we languished then and we languish now. We're but dim remembrance in far-off Spain. A forgotten bastion in the brilliant, sunstruck Caribbean Sea.

\*\*\*

One person who escaped this land of penury was Alonso Ramírez, who first went to México and eventually to the Orient as a sailor and then captain, before being captured by pirates. Years later, this colorful figure was put ashore in the Caribbean, from whence he made his way back to México and told his story to Carlos Sigüenza y Góngora. From the account found in *Los infortunios de Alonso Ramirez*, we read: "Borínquen (San Juan de Puerto Rico) has long been celebrated for its delicious waters that refresh ships bound for New Spain, and the beautiful bay and the impressive sight of El Morro fort guarding it with towers and artillery. As in other parts of the Indies we also find a great spirit among its sons, though they're subject to corsairs' attacks...Today for want of gold, which gave it the name 'Puerto Rico' and for the vehemence of the hurricanes, the people live in poverty...At the age of thirteen I left as a ship's boy, having little interest in cutting wood to make ships as my father had done, determined to leave and seek my fortune."

\*\*\*

I heard many tales of the early years from my mother, Doña Mercedes. She and my father looked at their own disastrous situation and applied to the Royal Audience in Santo Domingo to emigrate there. To their great relief, the request was granted. My father's contract had not been properly honored, so there should have been no problem.

But Governor Bahamón was jailing and whipping people for trying to escape Puerto Rico, and this island seemed more penal colony than loyal outpost of Spain. He refused to give my father leave. Since he *was* the government, there was nothing to be done. And so Father continued to seek ways to subvert the tyrant's will and take his family away.

Luckily for Father, Bahamón also tried to crush Juan García Troche Ponce de León, grandson of Juan Ponce de León. To battle this overbearing dictator, don Juan García sailed to Spain to appeal to the Crown. Among the documents was my father's official protest. To the townspeople's relief, don Juan carried the day in Sevilla and Bahamón was sent to Cartagena de las Indias. Most unfortunate for that coastal city, and most fortunate for San Juan! When don Juan was reinstated and the new governor appointed, Father's fortunes improved considerably, and he decided to stay. He seemed bewitched by this island, so seductive in promise, beautiful to behold, treacherous in act.

From our point of view, at least two good things stemmed from that decision. In 1586, the English corsair Francis Drake burned Santo Domingo and killed many. Had we moved there, I may not have lived to write this. That was one piece of luck. And that same year I met my husband to be in San Germán. But I get ahead of myself...

"He who retreats does not flee."
*No huye el que se retira.*

-Miguel de Cervantes y Saavedra,
*Don Quijote de la Mancha*

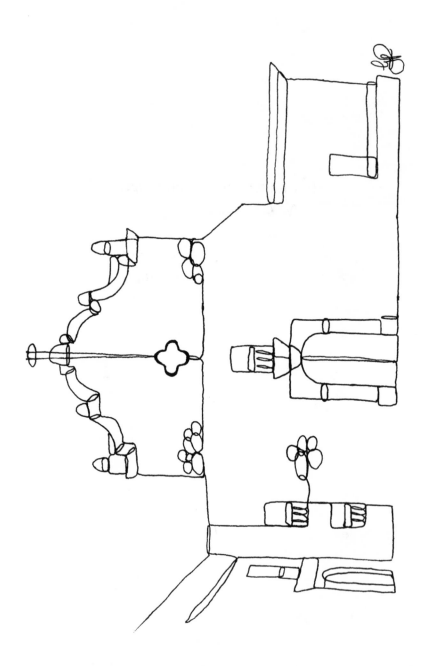

# Chapter Four

🙣 • 🙡

Feast Day, Santa Teresa 1578

Today is my saint's day. Though I am already 14 and truly a young woman, I was feted today as though I were a child. It was perfect. I was awakened early by the soft patter of a morning shower. The air was still quite cool. As I turned on my thick, much-mended linen sheet, I could hear isolated sounds of the coming dawn. A rooster's crow. The fluttery whirring noise of a dove as it flew from one tree to another in back of the house. The last burst of the coquí's night song. The little noises stood out in that abrupt silence that announces dawn in the tropics. The cacophonic sounds of a thousand night creatures ceased. Then came the stirring of our brave little settlement of fewer than a thousand souls, so grandly called a capital. I could hear the clip-clop of a horse, the opening of a casement window, the creak of a wood-hewed cart.

I'd begun to say my morning prayers, when the door burst open. In marched Mother and my three brothers, singing and clapping their hands. My sister, María del Pilar, and our Taíno servant, Margarita, who share the room with me, woke up with a start. I sat up in bed to receive the lovely gifts.

Mother gave me an embroidered silk handkerchief she'd done long ago as a girl in the great walled city of Ávila. In part I think this present was to nudge me to practice my own needlework, at which I'm not adept. Nor interested. My brothers gave me a braided leather bridle with a small silver bell to dress my pony, Reinita. Pilar handed me her long green ribbon I've long admired. Naturally, I'll lend it back when she wishes, as she's so often lent it to me. And Margarita, servant and almost-aunt (for her great-grandfather was a conquistador related by marriage to my mother's cousin), gave me a smooth polished green stone. It is in the shape of a coquí, the tiny tree frog that is a favorite symbol of her Indian ancestors.

Father appeared at the door with a hesitant smile and one of his precious books in hand. I almost wept when he gave it to me, one of his favorites and mine too: Seneca's *The Brevity of Life*. Only Father and I would think that title appropriate for a girl's saint's day. All the gifts are treasures I will keep forever. Except, perhaps, the ribbon.

We heard the church bell toll and everyone flew to dress.

Minutes later, we were picking our way through the potholes of Cristo Street. After a brief shower, our main road seems a muddy cow path. But following a storm, it seems a creek bed.

Though we hurried to the cathedral church, we were confident Mass would not begin without us. Mother was bringing the wine for the Eucharist, since the parish is always in short supply. She is generous by nature and always helps the beleaguered pastor. The bishop, of course, has his own wealth, but does not always share it.

Father says the island's economy is as bad as when we arrived fourteen years ago. We've had some help though. Mother has inherited a small pension from an uncle who died a wealthy bishop in México. With her help and the Crown's commitment, my physician father now owns several precious slaves to run his horse-powered small sugar mill, or *trapiche*.

On the banks of the Bayamón River, it is one of only eleven mills scattered here and there.

Depending on the weather, our family goes back and forth between our home in the capital and the hacienda which is really a rustic farmhouse just across the bay. Father, always depressed, still feels there is little future here and talks of leaving. Mother, a realist, says we never will.

Reluctantly, he's given his blessing to Francisco Javier to go to sea at first opportunity. My brother dreams of going to the Orient, reputed to be an exotic treasure house. So my favorite brother will leave us, no doubt to be followed by the others. María del Pilar married an officer from the garrison who died fighting Caribs, so she returned to live with us. Though she's beyond marriageable age now, she doesn't cease to look. She still dreams of escaping what she considers a disgusting backwater, and she is usually found idle, fanning herself and looking out the window.

Perhaps I'll end up running the mill with my husband, whoever he may be. Though supposedly we women don't enter commerce, in fact we often end up managing family affairs as husbands die or explore the world. And what about the world abroad? Queens have surely done as well as kings. After all, Isabel la Católica provisioned and led the troops in the siege of Granada, besides ruling Castilla and giving birth to many children. And today, that wicked woman Elizabeth rules heretical England and rewards her bloody pirates like Drake. Surely, I could manage a humbler enterprise like a sugar mill.

Look at our own family. My mother oversees our gardens in both homes. In the country, we harvest limes, grapefruit, pineapples, radishes, cabbages, lettuce, carrots, plantains, pumpkins, *yautía, yuca.*

Too, we have other fruits and vegetables and herbs. Bread we make from *casabe.* For meat, we now and then eat pork, goat and beef, and my very favorite, guinea hen. My brothers and I often dig for clams, pick oysters off the mangrove roots and at night hunt for land crab. One of my favorite dishes is *mofongo* – mashed plantain with garlic and a little pork, served with stewed land crab in a dish we call *salmorejo.* Um! It makes me hungry just to write about it!

When we go to the hacienda, we often fish from the riverside and always catch something. Mother brings the surplus to town, to be sold by our house slave there. The food is in much demand.

Father, of course, cares for the sick and reads his learned tomes. Daily he goes to check the governor-general's health and pay his respects. Then he goes next door, to the little hospital between our house and the Palacio Santa Catalina and begins his day. There are always patients. Some are recovering from battle wounds. But most suffer from some tropical affliction: palsies, tumors, lockjaw, fevers and scabs. I know from reading his books that another ailment is called "the English disease," but cannot figure out exactly what it is.

But I digress too much. I was writing of my birthday. We finally arrived at the cathedral. Though the lovely Gothic design of the chapel is austerely beautiful, the church itself is shabby. The Negro slaves brought in to build and maintain it are dying of old age. Maintenance depends on the eloquence of the bishop to shake his rightful money – the *diezmos* – from the tax-collector's purse. Needy himself for the military garrison, the governor-general often finds a way to subvent this. And though the faithful help as they can or can't, they too look to their own needs.

The few benches were wet, rain drops still oozing from the water-soaked straw roof. Puddles stood on the stone floor. The rank smell of old, wet grass pervaded the church. We could see the bright azure sky through the gaps above. Short daily rains are followed by clear skies. When the rains are too fierce, Mass simply has to stop. This month the vigil lights haven't been burning, since there is no olive oil on the island. There are no bees here, so instead of lightly scented lovely beeswax candles, we must make do with ugly things made of rancid animal fat.

On the main altar is a large silver crucifix. No one seems to know where it came from, but it must be México. The altar is lustrous dark wood, rich mahogany from the tall forests here. At the side is a carved Santiago de Compostela – *el Matamoros* – on a rearing horse, poised to charge the Moors in battle. Patron saint of Spain, his cloak is red and gold. It's a beautiful carving, brought from Sevilla.

Once church was full, Fray Diego gave Mass, served by my youngest brother Anton who's still learning the Latin responses. Then the priest gave a short sermon about accepting our lot and using Christ and Our Lady as our guide. They listen to us whenever we seek them, even if we've been careless and mean the moment before, he said. It was a good sermon, and made me think he was talking directly to me. Fray Diego is an austere person, but just and kind.

Fray Diego de Salamanca is our new bishop sent from Spain. Like most recent arrivals here, he is horrified at the state of the people and the church. Many of the curates have concubines, and drink to drunkenness, and spend church money on gambling. Father and the bishop, both being sober, educated and bookish, have become confidants.

The bishop's niece Ana is my best friend, and she often accompanies him when he comes home to visit. We overhear the adults' conversations, so we are aware of events around us. At least somewhat, considering that at times a whole year goes by without a vessel bringing goods and news from Spain.

Yet no one doubts that the motherland prizes this island for its military importance. If the enemy nations of France, Holland or England controlled this port, they'd guard the very gateway to the Caribbean and New Spain beyond. We hear that fifty more soldiers will be garrisoned here, and there is talk of building up the fortifications next to the governor's house at La Fortaleza.

The beauty of this place helps me deal with the frustration I often feel, when hearing people constantly complain about living in such a godforsaken place. If I were a boy, I could hope to escape and see the world. Since physical liberty is impossible, I must find freedom within, in another way. At night I sometime dream I am a Taína woman, before we Spaniards arrived. Those dreams are so real, I feel the presence of their spirits and hear their chants...from Eden, before the fall...

\*\*\*

I have read Bartolomé de las Casas's story of Anacaona, the Taíno chief in Santo Domingo whom even her enemies called a "gracious, prudent woman of great intelligence and authority – *una absoluta señora*." Though she was good to the invaders, she went too far. She and the other women "gave themselves easily to the Christians and didn't deny them their bodies." In consequence, the conquistador Ovando led his men to butcher all her people – and in deference to her station, hang Anacaona.

How true is Sor Juana Inés de la Cruz's verse, about men who blame women for leading them sexually astray:

"False men, you who blame
the woman without reason
Not seeing that you are who causes
The temptation and the sin."
*-Hombres falsos que culpais*
*a la mujer sin razón*
*Sin ver que sois la ocasión*
*de lo mismo que culpais.)*

\*\*\*

Most bishops hate to be appointed to this post. They assume the miter as late as possible, and move on as quickly as they can. But Bishop Fray Diego is a good Augustinian. Since there were no ships sailing to the capital of Puerto Rico, he and his party (and of course, my friend Ana) joined a war convoy in Sevilla bound for México. The ship dropped the passengers on the south coast of Guánica, where they mounted horses provided by the settlers.

Lugging goods and provisions, they rode horses and burdened the mules, following the south coast. Starting the climb up the bone-dry foothills, they reached the mountain range where streams and woods flourished and stopped at the pass, a place with mineral baths the Indians called Coamo.

When Fray Diego saw how miserably the twenty-odd families lived there – like savages, I heard him say – he ordered a parish church to be built in Coamo and staffed. At last the people will have some solace in that wild place.

But Fray Diego hadn't counted on our new governor, Francisco de Ovando Messias. According to all the learned people, he has no intention of bringing civilization to this island. All he knows is war. Fray Diego ignored his objections and convinced the Council of the Indies of the need for the church. The parish of San Blas de Illescas is to be built in Coamo. As did the bishop before him, Fray Diego begged the king not to send more soldiers as governors, for they know nothing of trade and less of government. What they know, they practice. War with the enemy, and repression at home.

An example of the good and the bad is Governor Messias. When he learned of yet another attack on San Germán by French corsairs, he rode pell-mell to the rescue. The French are the scourge of the south coast, though as I've grown old I see the Dutch and English are no better. These Frenchmen invaded the port of Santa María de Guadianilla. And then, aided by a traitor within, they went inland to the settlement, where they burned and pillaged and stole the women. Amazingly, the brazen villains actually settled in. About 300 people, not counting slaves, lived there.

Messías gathered a squadron in San Juan. On horseback, through downpours, the party pounded and clopped its way south over the green, water-logged mountains. Once there, they beat the French and freed the women. At least the governor is a competent warrior, which is no small tribute in our dangerous age. Of course, they were going to save *women*. Soldiers especially prize women here, since there are so few of us.

Many men strike up liaisons with freed slaves and keep a family on the outskirts of town. Bastards abound, of course, but no one really seems to mind except for an occasional priest. And perhaps the mother.

The day following my birthday, a most exciting event happened. I shall always remember it. A ship arrived from México, bringing new faces and goods on their way home to Spain. As usual, the city tittered with gossip and festivities. Our house was, unfortunately, commonly immune to such activity.

Last evening, though, after sunset, Father brought home for dinner Fray Diego and a mysterious priest friend. As usual, Ana came along with her uncle to visit me. The men ate quietly alone, after my mother had greeted them. Mother was sewing in her room and paying no attention to us, so we were able to creep to the other side of the door and overhear the subdued conversation.

"Bartolomé, you go too far! You always have, ever since your book was published," said Fray Diego.

"Brother, we must go far. Otherwise we're not heard. Look what my first book and others since have done! People actually argue in the highest sphere about the way we act here in the Indies, instead of taking the bloodlust for granted as in earlier years. Do you really think that if I'd been totally reasonable anyone would have listened? Passion must join thought to move minds and souls."

We heard Father's voice. "You're right, of course. There is as much evil in man as good. Only those who speak out like Fray de las Casas make us see that reality. We prefer mindless comfort unless jolted out of it."

Ana and I looked at each other with awe.

This had to be the great Defender of the Indians, Fray Bartolomé de las Casas. Next to us! This dynamic Dominican preacher has spoken and written so eloquently that he's turned theologians against each other, and forced the Crown to pass laws forbidding mistreatment of the Indians. Even the cautious Cardinal Cisneros has listened to him. Governors fear and hate him.

Just last week, Father had promised to buy me de las Casas's famous book, *Brevísima Relación de la Destrucción de las Indias*. And here was the author himself! Everyone knows when the book was first published in 1552, it set Spain and America aflame in debate. Father said that Spain's enemies quickly translated and printed it, to blacken her name in America. As if the English or Dutch were kinder! They don't even care if the Indian is baptized or not. But they are heretics, so what can one expect?

We heard some murmuring, and then Fray Diego's voice spoke up. "Well, it's Bartolomé's arguments that make it dangerous for him to be in America now. We know there must be agents of powerful men, even in this little capital, who would gladly place a knife in his back after dark. I have no doubt our governor himself would like to see it done."

Then he said to las Casas, "Especially after you turned Chiapas on its ear, by refusing the sacraments to anyone who didn't financially make up to the Indians what he'd stolen. When you touch a greedy man's purse, you touch his heart."

We heard them chuckle and the wine glasses clink, as though in a toast. Then Father said, with emotion I'd seldom heard, "I am honored by your visit, Fray Bartolomé. And though your lessons don't apply to us in Puerto Rico, since the Indians have been exterminated...."

De las Casas interrupted, "Oh, not so, friend. At the beginning of my mission, I made the horrible mistake of suggesting that black slaves be used instead of Indians, since the Africans are more accustomed to harsh labor. Now I realize what a grievous error I made. Since then the black African slave trade has increased tenfold, and shows no signs of abating. Those miserable creatures are subject to the same abuse we at first gave mostly to the Indian. No, we owe the black the same respect we owe the Indian. No more slaves to America. Remember how we so looked forward to seeing America? As an Eden on earth."

We heard silence for a moment, and then a clearing of the throat.

His voice resumed, quavering. "I, as you must know, was one of the first sinners. With Ovando I helped massacre those innocents in Santo Domingo. I will spend the rest of my life repenting it."

Then we heard a sob. Bartolomé again. "May God forgive me! I am a murderer. All of them, black African and Indian, should be treated justly, not like beasts. They are children of God, just as are we. Their souls are as dear to God as ours!"

Ana and I looked at each other, amazed. No wonder they were hiding this priest's identity. What he was saying would sound like treason to our governor. Who knows what the Inquisitors would say...

Just then we heard Mother coming down the stairs. Ana and I quickly headed for the interior patio to sit in the light of the precious oil lamp there.

Mother's eyebrows rose quizzically. "Are you girls doing anything useful? You should take out the lute and practice singing, if you're not in the mood for sewing."

At least I was given an alternative to sewing, which I detested.

I love books and music and abhor needles! We picked up the instruments and started practicing a *villancico* for Christmas time. If we played and sang well enough, the famous guest might come to listen.

Perhaps our song and string were pleasant enough. Or perhaps the men were tired. At any rate, they did come to sit on the patio benches and join in with "Puer Natus en Bethlehem."

As our guests began to leave, and the priests were giving us their blessing, I thought of our part-Indian servant. "Please, Fray Diego, let me call Margarita to receive your blessing."

From his expression, he knew that Ana and I had been eavesdropping and learned who the other priest was. He smiled slightly and said, "Hurry along. Our guest must be aboard ship tonight, as they take off at dawn."

I shook Margarita from her bed, where she was already dozing. "Hurry, come with me and don't bother to dress," I hissed. "I'll explain later."

With a robe clutched around her, she entered the room. As Fray Bartolomé caught sight of her dark skin and straight black hair, his eyes widened. Father said, "Margarita is distant family, since her great-grandfather was my wife's cousin. She is also descended from a distinguished cacique of the Taínos."

Unused to being the center of attention, Margarita nevertheless maintained her usual composure.

With a slight bow, Fray Bartolomé said, "I'm honored to meet a descendant of this land's first people. Let me give you all God's blessing."

We knelt and it was done. The visitors left, and I walked back with Margarita to the room, explaining about Bartolomé de las Casas.

"Of course, I know who he is," she said. "Do you think I of all people would be ignorant of his work?"

Chastened by my own presumptuousness, I went to bed. And dreamed of long ago, when the Indians roamed their homeland without fear of the white man. The next day I would ask Margarita to tell me some more tales.

"For liberty and honor, life must be risked."
*Por la libertad, así como por la honra,*
*se puede y se debe aventurar la vida.*

-Miguel de Cervantes y Saavedra,
*Don Quijote de la Mancha*

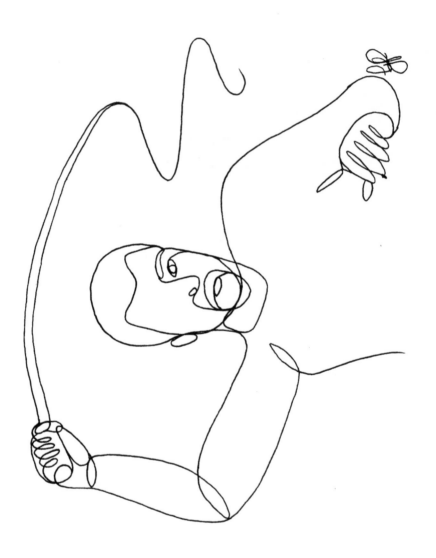

## Chapter Five

❧ · ❧

Fray de las Casas has quoted the sermon which first helped to convert him to the Indians' cause. It was Antonio Montesinos, the third Sunday of Advent in 1510, at the cathedral in Santo Domingo. He said, "We are the voice of Christ crying in the desert of this island...This voice tells me that all of you are in a state of mortal sin because of the cruelty you show the innocent population. Tell me, with what right, in the name of what justice, do you subject the Indians to such a cruel and terrible slavery? Are they not men? Don't they have a soul like any rational being?"

Four years later, the friar finally changed his own life and dedicated all to the Indian. He was preparing a sermon in 1514, he said, meditating on Chapter 34 of Ecclesiastes in the Old Testament. It starts, "A man of no understanding has vain and false hopes, and dreams give wings to fools. As one who catches at a shadow and

47

pursues the wind, so is he who gives heed to dreams...."
This was the moment of understanding for him. He gave
away his rich lands to an astonished friend, and began a
new life.

In Spain he won the ear of King Carlos's regent, Cardinal
Cisneros. Together with Montesinos and Palacios Rubios
he wrote something compared to Thomas More's *Utopia*.
It recommended that the system of *repartimientos* (distri-
bution of Indians to the Spaniards) be abolished.

But such was not to be.

In spite of Fray de las Casas's work, throughout Tierra
Firme the Indians work the fields and mines against their
will. In Puerto Rico and Santo Domingo, there's no problem. No Indian settlements even remain.

***

1582

This Sunday, the church was more than half full, as
usual, including a couple of lazy dogs who seemed to
prefer sleeping in the cathedral portico to any other spot
in town. My mother quickly gave the wine to the acolyte,
who took it back to the sacristy. That part of church is
very old and lovely.

It and the little chapel next were built by our first
bishop, Alonso Manso, more than half a century ago.
They have high gothic ceilings, beautifully executed in
adobe brick, with stone carvings. Ana tells me her uncle
heard about its beauty even in Spain. Of course, Bishop
Manso was from the University of Salamanca, as is the
present bishop, so perhaps our cathedral is famous only

in that city. But to achieve fame in Salamanca is perhaps sufficient. Father also studied there, and never ceases speaking of its beauty and brilliance. I sometimes wonder how someone of his sensibilities can stand life in Puerto Rico, so poor and primitive compared to that distant star of intellectual life?

On the other hand, oddly enough, my mother and I seem to thrive in what Father calls the "forgotten island, orphan of the Crown." Of course, I've never seen anything else. But even though I hope to see the world – and so I will! – this is still beloved home for me. And Mother, a privileged daughter of Ávila, also seems fond of this green-covered, damp rock, tossed by God into the blue Caribbean. In fact, it's really she and I who look after the garden and invent new ways to build and fix up the house in the capital and the hacienda in Bayamón. Mother is not too expressive in her words. Her acts, though, speak volumes.

Here I write in my journal, as though to sort things out by seeing letters on the page. I must have inherited Father's need to articulate and, thank God, Mother's sense of determined optimism. She often quotes something by an English nun that perfectly captures the essence of her own spirit. Dame Julian of Norwich, it was. She said, "All shall be well, and all will be well, and all shall be well." As though to say – whatever happens, so be it. *Deo gratia.*

I wonder if, as time goes by and I begin my own family and particular set of troubles, I'll have that same equanimity.

To return to this morning...Though Mass is held else-where too, the cathedral draws the biggest crowd. It's in the middle of town, on Cristo Street, just down from the big Dominican monastery and San José Church, and around the corner from the governor's residence at La Fortaleza. The small choir sings Gregorian chant, led by the acolyte who studied music in Sevilla. Many of the voices are young boys of mixed blood, who also study at the cathedral school and will likely enter religious life.

Today as always, carefully dressed if not silk-garbed, ladies and their servants and slaves are there on time. Some government officials arrive late, thereby signifying their own importance and reluctant compliance with the church. (I'm sounding as skeptical as Father!) But, too, many come who have no one to impress – just to offer up their day to Christ, receive the Holy Eucharist, and pray for strength.

We can't deny there's constant push and shove between civil and church leaders, especially those who deal directly with money. (Even Mother says when money enters the picture, virtue becomes a poor stepsister.) The church needs taxes through the mandatory tithing.

Called *diezmos,* the funds are collected by those who work for the government. Without money, the church can't run hospitals and schools and feed the poor. If the bishop is greedy, of course, he may enrich himself. There's also the governor vying for the same pot, and who so often wants the *diezmos* collection for military use or his own pocket. That's always been the way here. Conflict and greed.

Ana's uncle, the bishop, told her that Bishop Manso faced the same situation – even worse. He almost starved before finally returning to Spain on borrowed money. Then he was able to sort things out and return with more power – the post of the Grand Inquisitor of the Indies. He took sweet revenge on the governor, sending him back under arrest. In Spain the once-powerful governor died in a jail of the Holy Office. No wonder that lukewarm believers from the governor's office now make a point of showing up for Mass at the cathedral!

Though our bishop is also an Inquisitor – and therefore to be feared by all – he hasn't pursued heretics or backsliders in the faith. Like Alonso, he's more interested in using his power to assure government cooperation. In fact, how could there be real heretics here? The crown forbids the entry of colonists from other countries. Even slaves brought from Africa are forbidden to be Muslim, so they can be Christianized without reluctance. So – lazy, venal, or cruel, we may be. But in Puerto Rico we are all Catholics, bad, good, lukewarm, hypocritical and devout.

Mass attendance has another plus. It can be an opportunity to find a mate.

Not enough men of any class or condition exist to work the fields and plant and cut and process the sugarcane. Slaves are expensive.

What freeman would want to work as a slave in the brutal hot sun, bitten by insects, weakened by illness? With little or no work, he can survive by eating the fruit from the trees and catching guinea hen from the woods.

In Puerto Rico, it is said that the slaves and the free blacks and those of mixed blood outnumber the Spaniards.

I know my own parents are concerned about my meeting a proper man to wed. Most women of our station prefer to remain spinsters or to join the convent rather than marry beneath them. If you see what kind of life often awaits them – drudgery or utter boredom or abandonment – you can applaud their choice. And then a woman in the convent can lead a respectable and productive life. If she develops a true religious vocation, she may even lead a happy and fulfilled one.

But I already have a husband in mind. He doesn't know it. Eight years older than I, he has a manly, strong bearing. He's neither pretty nor coarse, but well put together. I know he has land in San Germán, in the southwest, but now and then he comes to the capital. He's a widower, they say. In church today, I saw him looking at me. I looked back, with interest in my eyes but properly serious even so... Tomorrow I'll ask Mother about him.

My dear friend Ana was also looking for possibilities at Mass. She likes a cousin of the governor who serves on the staff at La Fortaleza. He doesn't impress me at all. It's not his looks, for he's rather attractive in a poetic sort of way – tall and slender, with longish dark hair, and huge black eyes. But those eyes reflect greed and ambition. His bearing is over-proud, as though he were an emperor or a great *cacique*, rather than a hanger-on at his uncle's table. His fine clothes belong more at court in Spain than in this shabby place.

Poor Ana! Perhaps it's because she's been reared in a bishop's household and seen too many haughty men treated with respect there. She confessed to me she's been looking at this Manuel de la Vaca with interest for several weeks. He does her no courtesy in return. When he does deign to let his eye rest upon her, it's with such calculation that my blood runs cold.

***

Sor Juana Inés de la Cruz wrote convincingly about one of her reasons for choosing the veil rather than marriage. "...all of the little impertinences of my temper inspired me to wish to live alone; not to be bothered by others who would dig into my freedom to study, nor society rumor that would chatter and distract the marvelous silence of my books."

I fully understand her thought.

Already 20 and still not married, I am considering the convent. I love books and freedom, and shun the nattering and pretense of our small society. Just as did Juana de la Cruz, though I don't have her brilliance. Society bores me.

And just as the island shrinks in population, so does our family. My beloved mother died last year of measles. María del Pilar, my older sister who'd been widowed, married a lawyer of the Crown and moved with him to Cartagena de las Indias.

My favorite brother, Francisco Javier, took to sea six years ago. His last letter arrived two years ago, from the

Philippines. He said an Italian Jesuit named Mateo Ricci asked him to join him in China.

Imagine being at the court of the Mandarins! Since then we've heard nothing. God alone knows where he is today, or even if he still lives. If he ever saw that strange world...One thing is certain. A man of honor such as Francisco Javier is never lost on this earth.

Very early in the morning, I often attend Mass at the Dominican convent, and take the friars some produce which they in turn give out daily to the poor. Then I work in the garden together with my slave Tomás, who sells the excess in the marketplace along with the produce from his own patch. We have a mixture of the tubers cultivated by the Indians, like sweet potato, *yautía, malanga, ñame* and *yuca,* and the wonderful hot peppers. But we also have onions and cabbage. Our fruit trees that Mother brought to San Juan from Andalucía – lime, sour orange, and grapefruit – give just a little more than we use ourselves. Our *mayordomo* at the sugarmill is supposed to cultivate and harvest those fruits in the country, but unless I'm there to supervise, not much gets done in that regard. I try to go there twice a month, just to keep an eye on things, as well as to have good long horseback rides along the riverbanks.

Tomás is a hard worker and good person. I trust his judgment about many things. Brought to the island from the west coast of Africa when he was but a child, he's been with our family ever since I can remember. He was from the Yoruba tribe.

The Yorubas and Ibos are probably the most common African tribes on the island. Within a year or two, he'll have enough to purchase his freedom and build his own little hut in Puerta de Tierra, where many of the *mestizos* and free blacks have their homes. Then he'll find a wife, either from that neighborhood or the country, to have a family. He's tall and strong, can read and write and do numbers (thanks to me). Since he knows about farming and marketing, he'll probably have his choice of women seeking a kind and hardworking mate, be she black or white.

I hear that some freed slaves are making for the area of Cangrejos. Escaped black slaves from Spain's enemies are allowed to settle there on accepting baptism into the Church, and now free blacks from here are joining that settlement. For selfish purposes, I hope Tomás chooses Puerta de la Tierra so that he may easily help me in the garden. He knows as much about fertilizing and planting as does a Benedictine herbalist.

***

After a couple of hours rummaging in the clean rich earth of my garden, I go inside for a quick sponge bath and a cup of orange tea. Then sit for a while to read and meditate while awaiting the arrival of five young girls I'm giving rhetoric and basic Latin to. (Boys take classes with the friars.)

In the afternoon, after a light lunch and siesta, my friend Ana and I meet for a while, sometimes to talk and sometimes to play the *laúd* and sing.

My poor friend has a most unhappy life, for she married the vain man she cast eyes on in church so many years ago. His name is Manuel de la Vaca, and truly, he is well-named, for he has the intelligence and sensitivity of a cow! He lacks the tranquility of the beast though. He finally noticed Ana when his own position was in jeopardy, and he was afraid she'd move on to México with her uncle's family, taking with her a small inheritance. Though the bishop counseled her against the match, saying de la Vaca was lazy and shiftless, Ana insisted.

Now the bishop – her uncle and mentor – is gone, and she is left alone on this island with a spoiled and cruel husband. If not for Father and me, she would be totally at his mercy. And we are kept at a distance. To make matters worse – or perhaps, she would say better – she has a boy and a girl by him. The son is taking after her, all grace and light. And the daughter, sadly, takes after the arrogant father.

The other day I was at Ana's to dine. She'd been asking me for sometime, but I'd wanted to avoid her ogre husband's company. Finally, I realized that my refusal wasn't fair to her, and agreed to join them. She'd set the table beautifully with crisp white linen from Portugal, gleaming silver cups from México, and painted ceramic plates from Genoa. It was a feast for the eye. And then the meal! A delicious guinea hen roasted with sour orange and hot pepper. And fresh flat bread (*casava*) made from *yuca* on the side.

She'd also invited two young Benedictine monks, recently arrived from Nuestra Señora de Monserrate in Cataluña, on their way to join a monastery in México. Other than having to listen to gross Manuel's comments as he tried to ingratiate himself with the monks – he'd heard that one of them was a relative of the new governor – the meal was a success. Ana glowed with pleasure and doubtless was thinking that this sort of thing could give her some solace.

But the Benedictines left immediately after eating. I also was saying goodbye when an awful scene occurred. The little slave girl – she couldn't have been more than nine or ten – dropped one of the plates she was taking from the table. Though it didn't break, the rim chipped.

Ana's husband's face turned purple as his bile rose. His once smooth olive complexion had been attractive when she'd first laid eyes on him. But frequent visits to the brothel up the street must have given him a disgusting disease, and bequeathed on him the pox marks. His agile figure was already turning corpulent, as he stuffed himself like a sausage each time he sat at table. In sum, the indulgence of all his senses was taking its toll.

"You there, idiot!" he bellowed at the fearful girl. "Just stay there and await your punishment!"

The child quivered as he stormed from the room. In a second he was back, horsewhip held high. He lashed her hard across the face and raised his arm. Then he lashed her again, yelling, "Keep this up, and I'll make mincemeat of you! I'll brand your forehead, if you don't use your brains and stop breaking things! And then I'll sell you to the brothel!" Once again he lifted the whip.

I looked at Ana, who looked almost as fearful as the slave girl, so there was nothing else to be done. I rushed to the girl's side and held her, saying "Do that again and I'll report you to the Inquisitor! And I'll have my father back me up with his friends from Salamanca." We all well know the cabal at the University is powerful within both church and civil authorities.

"You wouldn't dare, not even you, the most foolish, over-lettered woman in Christendom!" he snarled. But he held back from lashing. The thin braided leather strip hung at his side.

"But I would, and you know it! If I make an official complaint, be sure it will be well-documented. You won't squirm out of it with your usual sliminess. You know that slaves have some few rights under the law. And you certainly haven't honored them. I've noticed that you've had this child working all day Sunday and missing catechism and Mass. You mend your ways or you'll be fined so heavily, you'll end in prison. Others far greater than you have landed there."

Ana had told me about his vicious behavior with the child and the other slaves, but that she didn't dare cross him or he'd turn on her.

Manuel de la Vaca looked at me with those hard, flat black eyes that I swear had been plucked from a viper. "Leave! Get out of my sight!" he shouted at the child.

Then his voice dropped a decibel in volume. It sounded like a serpent's hiss. "And you – do not ever set foot in this house again! Ana, you are forbidden to ever see this so-called friend of yours. And you'd better comply, or..." Then he turned on his heel and stalked from the room.

To his back I called, "I'll be watching this child to make sure she's at Sunday Mass and in good health! Don't try to get away with anything!"

Ana stood there motionless. Her small son approached her, and silently put his arm around her. The little daughter said nothing, sitting at the table to finish a second helping of *flan*. Was she smiling? Poor Ana.

Ana and I quietly hugged each other good-bye, and I took my leave. Since then I haven't seen my dear friend, except at church when we greet each other. On special occasions such as my saint's day or Corpus Christi she's sent a little note asking me not to abandon our friendship, that someday things will be remedied. I can't answer her, in case her husband might intercept the message. But I trust that all will work out – if only God would strike the monster with a musket ball or the plague or send him off to be killed by pirates! Until such a moment, I haven't much hope.

I must keep in mind the words of Cervantes, "God bears with the wicked, but not forever."

Even so, I've lost the company of my dearest friend, and must rely more on Father. Fortunately, he occasionally brings home visitors who are passing through, especially if they're from Salamanca or are also physicians. So that way, I do hear some small news of what is happening in the larger world, beyond this little island I call home and increasingly must think a prison. The men find it easy to leave and travel. But I must consider all this carefully, and how to break the bonds. If only I could go to México, and perhaps join my brother Antonio Blas. They say the level of learning and music and civilization there is as high or higher than in Spain. And they have the Indian culture, which father's visitors tell us is so rich and fascinating, and of which almost nothing remains in Puerto Rico. Words here and there. Food. Some old stories from the days of the conquest.

I hate this festering little community, where there's no escape. Oh, for freedom!

"the Spanish said… surely, these people (the Indians) were the most blessed of the world, if only they knew God."

*Los españoles dijeron… cierto, estas gentes (los indios) eran las más bienaventuradas del mundo, si solamente conocieran a Dios.*

-Bartolomé de las Casas,
*Brevísima relación de la destrucción de las Indias*

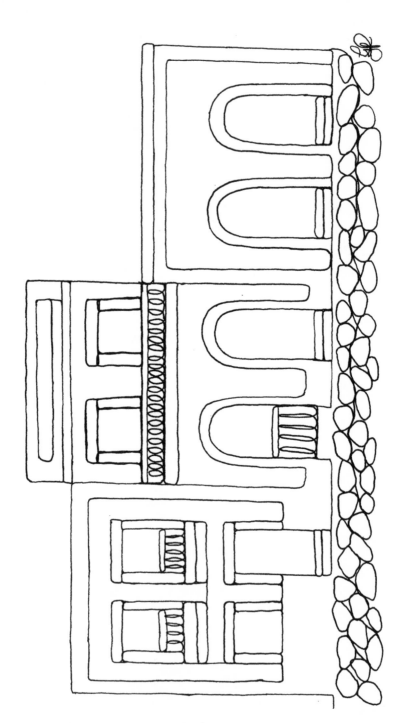

# Chapter Six

❧ • ❧

*1650*

*What heart-riven days were those. I read the words from those times and can almost feel that same cold fatalistic air.*

*How do pretensions rub raw any sensibility... Our society in Puerto Rico is a house of gaudy shells, mismatched and hollow, moldy. Only fools and evil ones like Manuel give worldly power such importance and exploit it. Even so, after having seen the extravagance and brilliance and crushing of the weak that are México, I know the very nature of society is to dazzle and impress. And to crush. So it has ever been. And ever will.*

Bishop Damián López de Haro said it well. When bishop of Puerto Rico, he wrote a poem. Not too long later, he was dead in that same "little islet".

"This is, madam, a little islet
lacking provisions and money,
where the blacks walk around in skins
and there are as many people in Sevilla's jail
as here the nobility of Castilla.
In few houses, many gentlemen
all trafficking in ginger and hides
these Mendoza, Guzmán and the Padilla.
There is water in the jug if there is rain
A cathedral church, but few churchmen;
Beautiful ladies lacking grace,
but bearing ambition and envy.
Much heat and coconut shade,
and best of all, a breath of air.
(-*Esta es Señora una pequeña islilla*
*falta de bastimentos y dineros*
*andan los negros como en esa en cueros*
*y hay más gente en la cárcel de Sevilla.*
*Aquí están los blasones de Castilla*
*en pocas casas, muchos caballeros*
*todos tratantes en xenxibre y cueros*
*los Mendoza, Guzmanes y el Padilla.*
*Ay agua en los algibes si ha llobido,*
*Iglesia catedral, clérigos pocos,*
*hermosas damas faltas de donaire,*
*la ambición y la envidia aquí an nacido,*
*mucho calor y sombra de los cocos,*
*y el mejor de todo un poco de ayre.)*

September, 1586

My second brother, Antonio Blas, is a good and studious person by nature. Father sent him to Santo Domingo where he studied at the Universidad de Santiago de la Paz. From there he went to Spain.

In Valladolid in Castilla, he entered the seminary and became a Dominican priest. After considering being a Jesuit, he decided against it. Too many of the Company of Jesus die as martyrs.

Then, last year, Antonio wrote to say he was en route to Nueva España to teach scripture and logic at the renowned Royal and Pontifical University of México. Father and I feel proud of his accomplishment in many ways. Especially Father. For the University of México, founded in 1533, has all the privileges of the world's most prestigious university, Salamanca, where Father studied. The only real New World rival is San Marcos in Lima, though other colleges exist. We were happy for Antonio and prayed that his ship would not fall to the French and English pirates who prowl our seas looking for Spanish vessels.

My youngest brother Rodrigo, always a wonderfully happy person who cheered up the family, stayed in Puerto Rico to help Father run the sugarmill. He died last year from typhus.

Now only Father and I are left. Both of us are depressed and lonely. We play chess and follow the book by Ruy López, *Libro de la invención liberal y arte del juego del ajedrez*. We discuss the stimulating ideas of Thomas More about man and Utopia, and read Vasco de Quiroga. One of my favorite books is *La Araucana* by Alonso de Ercilla. He relates what he himself has lived, in fighting the most unyielding Indians of the realm, in Chile. But this poem is even more: mythology, classics, love, fantasy, history. I read it again and again. The story of the Indian before the Spaniard is eternally fascinating. For that reason, the stories of the great poet el Inca Garcilaso de la Vega, son of conquistador and Incan princess, are lustrous as old gold and mysterious as the Andes themselves.

Then too, I play the *laúd* and teach reading and writing to a group of girls. I work in my garden. And I do the estate books and oversee the sugarmill. I pray. I do not know if God listens. But I take heart from Mother's distant cousin, Teresa de Jesús. In her books she describes how the soul can seem dry for years, how prayers seem but rote, how faith falters. I hope I can persist, for my soul feels sterile. Without passion of the spirit, what is life worth?

Books and mind are not enough, though I daily thank God my parents attended to my education. Learning is a joy. Yet I feel hollow. It is hard not to dwell on the absence of Mother and all the rest. I've about abandoned hopes for a husband and children. Since I would only accept one I could respect, the choices are slim, slim indeed... My girlish dreams are banished.

\*\*\*

I read with some relish the aphorisms of Baltasar Gracián, that wise and worldly Jesuit. This is one that gives me some comfort: "Enjoy a little more and strive a little less. Others argue to the contrary, but happy leisure is worth more than drive, for nothing belongs to us, except time, wherein even he dwells who has no habitation. Equally infelicitous is it to squander precious existence in stupid drudgery, as in an excess of noble business. Be not crushed under success, in order not to be crushed under envy: it is to trample upon life, and to suffocate the spirit. Some would include hereunder knowledge, but he who is without knowledge, is without life."

***

Our city has become a military bastion. With reason, I suppose, since Drake and Hawkins and all those English heretics like nothing so much as to kill a Spaniard. We surely need protection. But that means that most of the garrison in San Juan are crude soldiers whose lot in life is to fight and little else. They often take *mestiza* or *mulata* women as concubines, since their poor salary cannot sustain a proper family. Because of the situation, though, all suffer. The women who are concubines have a hard life with soldiers who feel only a temporary bond. The women and children are often abandoned, as the soldier is transferred.

Finally, just for a change of scene, Father has decided that we will travel to San Germán. A childhood friend of my mother's, a widow named Doña Enriqueta Guzmán de Villalobos, has invited us to come and stay at her house. She wants Father's counsel, as her only son is in

Nueva España. Mother used to describe her friend as a beautiful and charming woman, which doubtless has influenced Father's decision to travel. For several days my maid Margarita and I prepared food that would travel well. A bag full of the cassava, the flat bread made from yucca, of course. It was a staple of the Taínos – Margarita's people – and saved the first Spaniards from starvation when they still had not cultivated anything themselves. It's a most curious tuber. The poison variety of yucca is put in a woven basket-like tube, which is squeezed until the juice runs out. Then the yucca may be eaten if properly squeezed dry. Such a risk has never appealed to me. Surely life offers enough excitement without seeking out possibly poisoned food. I find it amazing that the Indians whom we consider so ignorant learned such a mechanism to detoxify a food. In a bad harvest of the domesticated variety, they knew they could turn to yucca brava.

To make the cassava, we grate the non-poisonous yucca that was brought from Spain. We make it into a paste and then fry or bake it. The Indian women, according to Margarita, cooked it on top of a hot stone. The bread emerges crispy and able to be saved for months. As a special delicacy for our journey, we salted some sardines Tomás caught in the bay, and even a nice cut of manatee. Boiled later in a tomato and pepper sauce, they would provide for several meals. Of course, we boiled guinea hen eggs and packed orange leaves to make tea on the trail, as well as oranges themselves, for juice. Dried rice and beans completed our supplies. We knew we'd probably find some wild fruit like *guayaba* and *jobo* on the way. And if fortunate, we might encounter a wild pig or goat the men could shoot and salt down to take as a present to our hosts in San Germán.

As a gift to the widow, we're taking a bolt of fine linen. Accompanying us are Margarita, two all-around workers from the sugarmill and Tomás, who has accompanied Father on this same trip before. A priest is coming with us, sent by the bishop to make a report on conditions of San Blas Illescas or Coamo, and on Porta Coeli in San Germán. Yet another person in the party is a Catalán merchant, newly arrived in Puerto Rico, who wants to look over the trading possibilities throughout the island. I fear he will quickly lose interest. The only real commerce is in mules, cattle, skins and wild ginger – and all that's mostly illegal to trade outside of San Juan.

Father left his *mayordomo* in charge of the mill on the Bayamôn River, and said we'd be back soon. Who knows though, how long we'll take? We simply closed up the house in San Juan, said our goodbyes to our few good friends, and left.

\*\*\*

We packed up the mules, saddled the horses, and rode off for the mountains. How wonderful to be leaving the stifling atmosphere of the city. And at last, a chance to see the *cordillera* and south of the island.

After a half day's easy ride on the trail, we reached the valley called Caguax by the Indians and made camp next to a lazy stream. That night we heard wild dogs baying at the moon. They were large and vicious mastiffs, having been bred to hunt runaway slaves, called *cimarrones*. Now they hunt whomever or whatever they wished, though wild pigs, goats and cattle generally suffice. They must have eaten enough, for they stayed clear of us, though I once caught a glimpse of these mean, wild creatures.

The only real inconvenience on the trip was rainstorms. Twice we were pelted badly, and had to stop riding and huddle together. Then it was too wet and slippery to ride, and we made a forced damp stop overnight. The next day we waited to ford a swollen river, and then cautiously worked our way across.

Up in the green, luxuriant mountains, we finally reached the pass called Coamo. It was the sixth day. We pitched our tents in the flat area between the river and the springs, both horses and riders grateful for the rest. My sturdy mare, the daughter of my old Reinita, has a steady, comfortable gait, as fast as a trot, but not as bumpy. It's a fine gait or *paso fino* that's being trained into the island's horses, perfect for going up and down steep hills.

Margarita tells me the Taínos used to come here for therapeutic baths and stay days. I do prefer following the Indian custom of bathing daily, rather than the Spanish custom of bathing monthly at best! None of the men in the party wanted to use the springs, but I insisted to Father that Margarita and I would bathe in the warm, bubbling waters. There are rocks scattered around the site, so she and I simply went off from the group, undressed, and lay for hours in a pool. Fortunately, we made camp there that night, so we could indulge ourselves. Our tiredness simply floated away – down to the river, down to the sea. The problems of San Juan seemed from another lifetime.

On the trail again, Father admitted to me that he'd tried the waters too. He said as a medical doctor, it would be an ignorant act on his part not to experience what the Indians claimed was so good for the body. And of course, he liked it!

We rode down the mountains and reached the plains of the south coast. It was terribly dry, much different from the lush north. But the lack of thick vegetation made riding far easier. We speculated among ourselves what we'd find in San Germán. Three years ago, Captain-General Diego Menéndez de Valdez received expensive clothes from Spain for his own use. But his soldiers were so hungry that he went all the way to San Germán to trade his finery for cassava, meat and corn. Few people do as our family has always done in cultivating an extensive garden. I will never understand why, since the garrison is always hungry.

Since little coin circulates here, we generally use barter to exchange goods and service. Even the bishops are paid in sugar and cowhides. In earlier days, monies from Santo Domingo and Cartagena were destined to fund our island. But they never did arrive. Though México is so rich, our condition remains the same. Our *situado* from there is often lost at sea to storms and brigands.

Surely, México must be richest place on the face of the earth. And the most pleasant. How I would love to go there, and flee this island...

We arrived at Nuevo San Germán, consumed with curiosity to see this old settlement which traditionally has defied San Juan officialdom. Today the brave community also defies constant attacks by French corsairs and pirates. It is laid in the hills, inland from the sea, and has no fortress. In the center of the town is a well-designed plaza and a lovely, well-proportioned church called Porta Coeli. A boy from the town showed us the way to the widow Doña Enriqueta's home, about a league away.

As our party rode up the broad path lined with flowering jasmine, we admired the graciousness of the hacienda. On masonry stilts, the small main wooden house perches above a flight of stairs. Its roof is designed to catch the water, with *cuatro aguas* or four slopes. On the broad covered porch that goes around three sides hang hammocks for siesta time and casual overnight guests.

Doña Enriqueta came out to greet us. Dressed in pleated white skirt and bright red blouse with shawl, she looked happy and vivacious. She was rather stout now, but still had a pretty face with smile lines around the mouth.

Father dismounted, kissed her hand, and all went well. She hugged me and commented that I looked like my mother. She offered us cool drinks of *mabí*, made from the bark of a tree. Delicious and refreshing! Then she took us to our rooms to rest awhile and unpack our belongings. The mattress was packed with fresh straw. Straight away I felt more comfortable than I had for – well, years. Why, I don't know. I fell into a deep sleep for hours.

When I arose, I walked around the house and grounds.

There's a constant lovely breeze that blows here. Fresh. No city stench. There must be different plants here, and of course no neighbors, for the air smells far more fragrant than that of San Juan.

The servants and slaves live in little straw huts that look like Indians' *bohíos*. The kitchen and bathhouse and toilet are also in separate huts, each apart from the main house. The compacted dirt floor around this place is swept clean each day.

We gave the widow her gifts and felt delighted to plan for a long stay, at her request. Her son Andrés will be arriving sometime from México, and she wants us to meet him. We quickly agreed and got into a nice routine of riding, eating, sleeping and visiting. Reading, of course, though we provided the books. The terrain is rather different from home, hillier and much drier.

San Germán el Nuevo exists because Governor Solís insisted all the settlers move inland for safety, about four leagues from the sea. They did it angrily, resenting officialdom's interference with their affairs. They complain bitterly about the new site: too hilly. Too far from the water source, the Guanajibo River. Too dusty a soil, a clay that blows in the wind and stains the clothing. Too this. Too that.

After resting a few days at the hacienda in Nuevo San Germán, we mounted our horses for another stage of the long journey, to camp near the beach where doña Enriqueta's son would arrive. In just a few hours we arrived at this brave little community on the mouth of the Guadianilla. It used to be called Sotomayor after its founder, who died in a Taíno assault that devastated the first settlement.

The story about that attack is fascinating. Leading the survivors from certain death was the famous Salazar.

His valor was so extreme that the Taíno leader asked him to voluntarily come to see him, so he could see the hero face to face. Though the other Spaniards understandably thought him mad, Salazar went to greet the *cacique*. And when the champion had finally taken the survivors of the attack at San Germán to Ponce de León at Caparra, about twenty leagues from San Juan, he was again greeted as a hero.

The legend of the valiant Salazar is wonderfully dramatic. Ponce took troops with him to attack the Indians, leaving Salazar behind in charge at Caparra of the infirm, the very old, the very young and the women. He was called, ironically, "captain of the crippled" (*capitán de los cojos*). But he led this motley group in a successful battle against the Taínos.

Now he became famous throughout the whole island – so much so, that the Indians taunted the other conquistadors with this phrase: "You're not Salazar, so I don't fear you!" (*No sois Salazar, pues no os temo.*)

Knowing these true tales made magical the moment of seeing the old settlement, which Salazar had saved so bravely. I had seen Caparra, of course, since it was not that far from our hacienda.

\*\*\*

The poet Juan de Castellanos published in 1589 the "Elegies of the Illustrious Men of the Indies," which included this:

> The brave Salazar blew the horn
> Calling all those at hand;
> He took as his band
> Boys, the lame and forlorn:
> But like demons from hell
> In strength and daring,
> From Caparra they went bidden
> By jagged mountains hidden.

> *El fuerte Salazar tocó su cuerno*
> *Llamando los que están apercibidos;*
> *Recogió los que son de su gobierno,*
> *Mozuelos medio mano y tullidos;*
> *Pero como demonios del infierno*
> *En ser fuertes, osados y atrevidos.*
> *De Caparra salieron y sus puertos*
> *Por ásperas montañas encubiertas.*

\*\*\*

Doña Enriqueta told us other tales as we rode to the coast. Since I'd never known anyone from my mother's youth, it was a sentimental experience to meet her. She spoke kindly to me, but directed a great deal of attention to Father...

My father seems attracted to the widow. Not that she's the young pretty thing as painted by Mother. Of course, that was Ávila more than thirty years ago. Now she's short and chubby rather than petite, carrying pure white hair in a bun rather than raven tresses, and just a bit bossy... Withal, she is kind, open and lively in manner.

Her *estancia* is vast. Understandably, lacking husband or sons to run it, her possessions have deteriorated. At the camp in the old hut, in Guadianilla on the coast, we await the arrival of her son. I bathe each day in the ocean waters at a calm inlet. A huge tame manatee lives there, so I'm well accompanied. Father, resigned, listens to doña Enriqueta's chatter. I think he rather enjoys it.

The son will decide with his mother what to do with the property. The poor woman has suffered cruelly. Years ago, her baby was snatched by the Caribs and never returned. Since those Indians are cannibals, the worst was feared. And several years ago, French pirates ran through one son with a sword and kidnapped a daughter, as they ransacked the settlement. Though the Villalobos were able to ransom her after several weeks, the poor girl was never the same. She died within the year.

I look forward to meeting the surviving son. Following the bloody attack by the Caribs, Andrés's father sent him at an early age to México to live with a friar cousin who taught at the university. After studying there, the young man married and worked at a silver mine for his wife's family. She died within months of her wedding, and he became something of a wanderer.

From everything I hear, I strongly suspect that he may be the one I noticed and liked at the Mass on my saint's day long ago at the age of fourteen. A century ago, it seems.

## Chapter Seven

November, 1586
San Germán

Let me describe how it happened.

He came ashore. A Viking. A bright sun shone, gilding his reddish-blonde wind-blown cap of curls into a golden halo. The piercing blue eyes and long high-bridged nose recalled his Galician forefathers. And the sense of acute intelligence and restless energy, I do swear, charged the very air around him. Used to the pessimistic, if kind, lethargy of my father, I was overwhelmed.

After kisses and hugs and introductions and ferrying his goods ashore by lighter, Andrés and the rest of us walked and rode to the old half-abandoned house on the coast. It seemed a welcoming procession for an exotic Arabian prince. Swarming about were old friends from around the countryside, the captain and officers from his ship the Santiago de Compostela, and of course our small party from San Juan. People streamed from their huts to greet him, dogs barked madly and children clapped and shouted huzzahs. All that was missing was the sound of church bells and trumpets and pennants flying in the breeze.

Though we hadn't killed a wild pig on our journey, Doña Enriqueta had been fattening up a big old sow for her son's arrival. Well-marinated in sour orange, *recao*, garlic, salt and oregano, it had been on the spit since before dawn, slowly turning above the charcoal embers.

The spicy, savory scent filled the air. I hoped pirates wouldn't smell it at sea, for they would surely attack us, just to eat the roasted pig. Resting on stones above other fires were pots of boiled green bananas and corn fritters and fried turtle eggs, all yolk. And the usual accompaniments of pig – its stewed innards, *mondongo* and *gandinga* – simmered nearby in a delicious broth, while the popular blood sausage or *morcilla* was already being gobbled up by the crowd.

It must have cost Doña Enriqueta a fortune, even though everyone seemed to have contributed something to the fiesta. Players of *laúd* and timpano and tambourines and drums struck up their music, and people began to dance.

Dusk fell early. But torches were lighted to illuminate the festivities. Shadows flickered in the light of the flames, and the music seemed to be echoing from the darkened hills behind and the expansive ocean beyond. Above, the gloriously-dark sky unveiled a thousand stars to shine on us, these few people clustered together on this spot of land surrounded by vast sea. It was surely the most emotionally charged evening of my life.

At first, I remained mostly with my father, who in turn was hovering happily next Doña Enriqueta. It was the first time I'd seen him smile since Mother's death. Of course, Andrés kept returning to our group. His mother kept up a constant flow of questions and information and "thanks-be-to-God" while Father and I looked on. Then Andrés would drift away to talk with friends, and drift back again.

For about two hours, this meandering rhythm went on, until people settled down to talk softly, eat constantly, and drink rum or *guarapo*.

Doña Enriqueta was wisely saving the demijohn of wine.

We'd brought it from San Juan for family consumption. Even so, it was apparent that people here had a larger variety of goods than we had in the capital. Everyone admits they trade in contraband with visiting ships, and thus avoid taxes.

Then Andrés strode directly towards me. He made a brief little bow and offered his arm. "May we walk?"

We could have been at the Plaza de Armas in San Juan on a late Sunday afternoon, so formal was his manner. I glanced at Father, deep in conversation with the widow.

"Of course," I answered.

We strolled around the fringe of the gathering. The light of a bonfire and the torches painted the scene a flickering yellow red against the black night.

He launched immediately into the most amazing conversation, with no preamble. "María Teresa, please believe me when I tell you that I've thought of you since spying you in the cathedral some years back when you were a young girl," he said. His voice was low and controlled, with the melodious lilt of México.

I couldn't hide my surprise. "What? We weren't even introduced! And I was only a girl!"

He chuckled. "Aha! You remember too!"

I blushed in the darkness. "Youth always notice those who are a few years older. It's nothing."

"No. It's something. Our eyes communicated – and in some small mysterious way, so did our souls. I asked about you and was told you were one of the few women who could read and write."

I held my breath.

"Also, that you were a budding intellectual, fearful to behold! But you were still very young, it's true. And I was an unstable young man, recently widowed and full of grief, preparing to leave again for Nueva España. I even asked the bishop, who was my cousin's good friend, to say a few nice words about me to your father, and also suggest that perhaps we could meet someday."

"Is that so?" I said slowly. "Father certainly never mentioned anything to me. But I should admit I did notice you, and perhaps even entertained a childish dream or two."

With that, Andrés took my arm firmly in his. And I most surely was willing. I could feel the muscles in his strong forearms. I liked it. Exceedingly so.

We stopped walking at a little rocky area near the river. It seemed a natural grotto, and the wind blowing up from the sea broke here. We heard the faint rush of river water coursing down to the sea. And – it must be my fervid imagination, I thought, overwrought from reading too many of those foolish novels of chivalry when I was young – the scent of jasmine seemed to hang in the limpid air. I'd tried to follow Teresa de Ávila's example and stop reading such silly things that only serve to disorient the imagination. But I enjoyed them still, nonetheless.

"This was always my favorite place around here," he said. "I insisted Mother plant jasmine, even though she said it wouldn't grow so near the sea. Can't you smell it?" He lifted his face to catch the fragrance.

"I'm not sure," I responded uncertainly. Actually, now that I knew it was real, I was telling myself to refuse the heady scent. And the sound of coursing water. And the touch of the humid air on my cheek.

Then his muscled arm on me. And, as though all that were not enough of an assault on awakened senses, the grandeur of the immense starry night sky. I would not allow myself to behave like some ridiculous girl, suddenly lovestruck over the first interesting man to make an approach. He was thirty years old, handsome, dynamic, and who knows what else. What skeletons might lie in his cupboard?

I couldn't help but remember one of Gracián's thoughts: "Know how to analyze a man. The alertness of the examiner is matched against the reserve of the examined. But great judgment is called for, to take the measure of another...Words show forth the mind, yet more his works..."

He might as well have read my mind. "But you, as I said, were young. I'd returned for just a few months to my birthplace of Puerto Rico, but then went back again to México. Finally, sick to heart with everything, I joined a community of Christianized Indians. I became more Indian than Spanish. And I lived with a wonderful Indian woman called María Isabel. And had two sons with her."

We continued to stroll in silence. What did he expect me to say? His life was his. And many men in this chaotic life that swept them here and there had fathered children by different women. Even our king, Felipe II, reputed saintly, had two bastards.

I said what I'd long been thinking. "I'd love to see México, and travel the sea. Tell me about your journeys."

Andrés suddenly detached my arm and expansively swept the air. "This is but a suggestion of what the sea and that far land are. Puerto Rico is small and lovely, surrounded by sky and water, but a land anchor. But when you are at sea, with only a small, rocking barque underfoot...

The sensation of being adrift in the immensity of space is overwhelming. There's no cave to hide in when the hurricane comes, no mortar fortress for protection. Only you and God and the weather. It's surely the most liberating feeling on earth. It's breaking the bonds of routine and man's company – except of course the crew that's occupying the same moveable space with you."

Interjecting, I said, "But part of why it's so extraordinary has to be that you have a destination. You're not in a state of endless wandering. That, on the contrary, I should think would cause despair. Imagine being one of those poor souls on a ship of fools, set to sea with other lunatics. You know, how towns in Europe banded together to provision a ship, and put aboard all those unfortunates who had no one to care for them. The ship would try to dock at a port, but would merely be given provisions if lucky – and forced to go on. What a sad pilgrimage to death!"

He looked at me and burst out laughing. "I'd heard you knew how to read and write well. Now I see you don't only read romances!"

"Of course not," I retorted. My favorites are Thomas More's *Utopia* and Erasmus's *In Praise of Folly*. Do *you* know them? And of course, Teresa of Ávila and Sor Juana Inés, and..."

He laughed again, and said, "Indeed I do, and I admire your choices. We'll have to discuss them at length later. But Bartolomé de las Casas is my favorite writer and thinker by far. Do *you* know him?"

"Yes. Yes, indeed," I responded.

My curiosity was piqued. "Who told you I could read and write?" Most men and women can read just to sign their names and the very basics.

"Why, Bishop Diego de Salamanca, your father's friend." Of course, Ana's uncle. "And what else, if anything, did His Lordship say?" I queried.

Andrés stammered, "To go away and leave you alone. That you were too young and I was too problematical. To come back when I'd grown up and so had you...."

What an intriguing situation this was. I had to know more. "And then?"

"A few months ago, I received a letter from my mother, beseeching me to visit her. As an incentive, since she somehow knew I'd asked about you back then, she mentioned she was inviting you and your father to San Germán at this time. She was sure he'd accept. Also, she said that you'd not married."

"And what of your Indian concubine? Did you just cast her off? And your two sons?"

Angrily, he shook his head. "She was what you call my 'concubine' because she refused to marry me, a Spaniard. She lived with me, and loved me, and bore me children. But she'd make sure she'd not be forced to enter the white man's world. María Isabel is intelligent and understanding, and knows the Spanish way. She knew that one day I'd perhaps wish to return to the world of my fathers, that the rest of my life would not be among her people. She didn't want any kind of coercement – whether legal or emotional – to have to abandon her own way."

"How then could you leave a woman you love?"

"I still love her in a certain way. Who could not? You will love her too. She's a good and noble person, and the mother of my two sons. But the sort of love to build a lifetime on? No.

I no longer want to escape to the Indians, and she couldn't live any other way. I don't blame her – it's the way things are. And she doesn't blame me, either."

He grasped my shoulders and turned me to face him. "So now you know much but surely not all about me. I want a good and bright wife, who will rear my children in my traditions, and I want a woman who is beautiful and moves my body and spirit. You."

Andrés started to pull me towards him. I pushed him away. Presumptuous fellow...but how powerfully attractive. "But..."

"I am an honest man, faithful to God, Our Holy Mother Church and to Spain. I have property and education, and I work hard. I will be a good and faithful husband to you, if you will have me. And you will love me..."

Christ's blood! I thought to myself, shaken and unsure to the core. Does this make any sense at all? What should I do? Is this the way things should be? Suddenly his mouth was on mine, and his hand was caressing my neck and then my body. At least one doubt was removed. It felt wonderful and made sense. I responded, and passion grew...

You, dear reader of this journal, need no more detail. Suffice to say, we have decided to wed three weeks from now. The return trip takes about ten days – depending on weather. Andrés will follow me to the capital after arranging matters at the family hacienda. It appears that we will live both in Nuevo San Germán and in Bayamón / San Juan, until we make up our minds which to dedicate ourselves to. I'm already predisposed to Nuevo San Germán, just to escape the cloying air of officialdom. We'll see how such an arrangement fares.

Meanwhile, a lawyer is drawing up the legal documents.

We both own personal property. What we acquire in marriage will belong to both of us. And, of course, children are forced heirs. Andrés will give his two *mestizo* sons their inheritance in life, and invest it for them in México, duly registered there. Since the establishment treats *mestizos* as inferior to Spanish and white *criollos*, he wants to assure the children have legal and economic standing.

Most pleasing to me is that we must go to México to make these arrangements. At last the opportunity to see that fabled land! We will stay perhaps six months to a year, so I must arrange for Father's convenience at our house in San Juan and our estancia in Bayamón. I had thought that perhaps he and Doña Enriqueta might have marital interest in each other. But Father in a confiding moment after two glasses of sherry said that though he enjoys her company and it would perhaps be economically beneficial to each, there's more to marriage than that. He remembers my mother too vividly, he said, to marry again. He did not specify further...

But my own life is taking a new path. Andrés.

And at last I will see the larger world. God willing...if we elude pirate and corsair and hurricane, our trip will be a great adventure. I hope it will in fact take place...

***

We were married as planned, three weeks after our meeting. But the much-anticipated trip to México did not yet take place. I suppose it was just as well. We had a hard time adjusting to marriage.

Andrés was accustomed to being waited on – immediately. "His lordship," I called him privately. I dare not think what he called me privately! Though attentive to my ideas, his were clearly more profound, more reasonable, and certainly his decisions were wise. On the other hand, I'd grown used to the freedom of solitude (but for my undemanding father's company) and answering to no one.

We were married in the Church, of course, Porta Coeli. There would be no escape. At least not for me. Luckily, our sense of duty was matched by a marvelous passion. Had it not been so, our union would have stifled in the drawing room, over conversation and coffee. Gradually, he came to accept that the reason a woman has an intelligence is to use it, not just to simper and serve. And I learned how to be accommodating and tried very hard to be gracious.

We began the arduous but engrossing task of putting both my mill and his hacienda into good working order. We work well together, now. For the most part.

Our former slave, Tomás, finally agreed to act as *mayordomo* for the sugar-mill, with the understanding that the two slaves there would be freed in two years if the hacienda made a certain profit from the sale of sugar and rum. We agreed, especially after having read the arguments of Bartolomé de las Casas against the whole concept of slavery.

Even worldly Gracián agrees, saying, "Know what is evil, however much worshipped it may be. Let the man of intelligence not fail to recognize it even if clothed in brocade or crowned with gold, because it cannot thereby hide its bane; slavery does not lose its infamy, however noble the master."

Andrés found a person who seems reliable to attend to selling.

His farm produces ginger, horses, cattle hides and salted meat in San Germán. His operations generate far more wealth than my father's and mine, but the management in our absence will ultimately decide the success of each enterprise. In Tomás I have no doubt. About the person Andrés has chosen, I'm not so sure.

The most thrilling event was the birth of Esteban after we'd been married three years. I'd had two early miscarriages before, and had begun to worry that I couldn't bear children.

Esteban looks rather like me, with dark hair and big dark eyes. But he has the robust build and agility of his father. He acts very like his father too – very energetic and outgoing, and with a sweet nature and strong character. A joy! We hope to have a big family, all of them as wonderful as Esteban. *Deo gratia!*

We made preparations for our long voyage. Margarita, my old maid from childhood, would oversee Father's comfort at the house in town and care for our first son Esteban. I left all accounts in order.

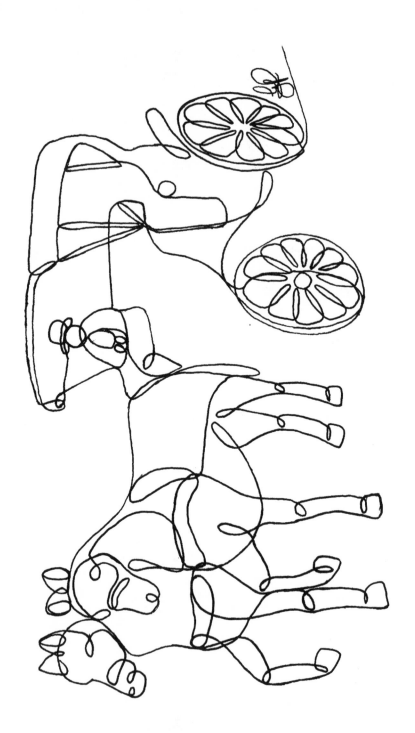

# Chapter Eight

July 26, 1590
Aboard the "Santiago de Compostela"

As I write these lines, we are at last bound for Nueva España. It is the very vessel that brought my husband Andrés to Puerto Rico four years ago. We had hoped to embark a few months after our wedding, but it was not to be. After the Santiago had returned to Spain, it was outfitted and provisioned. But not for trade. Goaded by Francis Drake's attacks throughout the kingdom, then by Elizabeth's beheading of her Catholic cousin Mary, Queen of Scots, our king Felipe II decided to attack England. Our ship's captain Raúl de Maldonado told us the story. I will try to be true to his words.

"For years, of course, the battle had been brewing. Aided by his queen, Drake has plundered, burned and ravaged Spain at each opportunity. Ever since Elizabeth's father Henry divorced Catalina, daughter of our own

Isabel and Fernando, and then persecuted the Holy Catholic Church, there has been enmity between the two countries. Soon after the beheading of Mary, Elizabeth allowed Drake to go up and down the Portuguese coast burning fishing villages – even the fishermen's nets, all their boats, everything. He torched all the ships in the Bay of Cádiz. Then it was on to Cape Saint Vincent where the English burned 1,600 to 1,700 tons of hoops and staves. Little did we know what an important and murderous event that would turn out to be.

Well, to make a long and sad story short, let me tell you how I saw it. About 130 vessels, great and small, gathered in Lisbon harbor. It was 1588. The head of the fleet was a good and able man, though much maligned afterwards: The Duke Medina Sidonia. Filled with zeal, we were assembling the invincible armada. Galleons of Portugal and Castilla made up the first line, and four galleases of Naples, strange but strong, swift ships that were half galleon and half galley. We, the Santiago, were in the second line together with other large merchant-men. The Biscayans were under my friend Juan Martínez de Recalde. There were men and ships from Guipuzcoa, Andalucía, Venezia, Raguso, Genoa, Sicilia, Barcelona. Fast small ships would act as scouts and couriers and slow hulks for supply vessels.

The battle began slowly, as one after another entered the fray. We fought a good fight. But so did they. Our main problem was lack of supplies and ammunition, but also the English ships were far more maneuverable than ours.

Halfway through the battle our men were weakened and sickened by rotten water and supplies. Remember Drake's attack on Cape Saint Vincent? We depend on tight-fitting casks to keep our water, salt-meal and biscuits fresh. But when our ships sailed from Portugal, they carried leaky, foul, green wood casks. The mature wooden staves had earlier been burned by Drake. Our fleet was battered by storm. Then it foundered on the shifting sands off Holland. We were in disarray. Our escape route was around the north tip of Scotland, then down the west coast of Ireland to Santander. Some ships tried to put in for water and repairs, but that wild and desolate coast of rocky cliffs churned to bits the shot-torn hulls and ragged rigging. Thousands of our men must have drowned there. At Galway, where we'd often traded wine with the Irish, the English were waiting to hang us and any Irishman who'd extend a hand.

The Santiago was fortunate. We were able to stock fresh water and supplies at Dingle Bay on our way home, unbeknownst to the English. But a hospital ship next us met a sad fate. Filled with wounded men and despairing of reaching Spain with any patients alive, she meant to head up the channel to seek refuge in a French port. She wrecked on the Devon Coast. Some men and all stores were taken by the English. Altogether we salvaged two-thirds of our fighting strength. It was not quite a debacle. But close.

We might learn from our king...

Just last year in his garden, after the defeat, he heard one of the monks say that God simply could not allow blighted fruit to grow on the much-tended pear trees that line the south wall at El Escorial. Felipe said sharply, 'Brother Nicholas! Mind what you say! It is impiety and almost blasphemy to presume to know the will of God. It comes from the sin of pride. Even kings, Brother Nicholas, must submit to being used by God's will without knowing what it may be. They must never seek to use God's will.'"

Our captain stopped a moment as though to brush a speck from his eye before continuing. "Our king is a man of steel: iron control, diligent, loyal to God and Spain. A man of honor. I am proud to serve him."

We were much moved by the captain's account. And more than ever, we realize that England is a constant threat. Drake and his queen now lust more than ever for the Indies. Governor-Captain General Menéndez de Valdes has been building up the fortifications in San Juan. A new fort at El Morro is rising. Menéndez claims it will be the mightiest fort in the Indies. Meanwhile everyone says that Drake and John Hawkins and their heretic queen even now are organizing a powerful fleet to attack the Indies of Spain.

All of this, of course, makes me rather fearful on this voyage to Nueva España. Yet, what joy to be at sea. It is the first time for me, since my mother gave me birth crossing the Atlantic. I, too, am now a mother.

August 4, 1590
The feast of Saint Dominic, founder of the Order of Preachers. At sea en route to México

On this ship are ten Dominican priests bound for México, destined later for the Philippines.

To celebrate the feast day, they organized a marvelous party. We all sang, with flutes, drums and one viola playing. I wish I'd brought my *laúd*. Then a gala banquet with fresh fish – *dorado* – and baked plantains and sugared guava with fresh goat cheese. After feasting, the younger ones, joined by a few other passengers, acted out part of that most marvelous work, *Lazarillo de Tormes*. How true and witty! I daresay people hundreds of years from now will still read and act it out. The group acted and spoke so well, that I cannot conceive the best theatre in Sevilla doing better...On the other hand, I've never been to Sevilla, so who am I to say?

To surge over the ocean was all I had hoped for. The infinite space of stars and water stir the soul. Since I was born at sea, I have an odd sensation of having returned home. Had I been a man, surely I would have been a seafarer.

*** 

September 1, 1590
Nueva España

At last we arrived, with no harm from pirate or tempest. At the port of Veracruz, we were offered lodging at the Dominican convent. The opulence was, well, scandalous. Even the governor in Puerto Rico could not match such luxury. Beautiful silk tablecloths, costly curtains and draperies, an abundance of fine china and porcelain, sweets and delicacies and the finest wines in excess. Only the library was inferior. The prior, director of this marvelous palace-hostel, was young, amusing and worldly. A wealthy younger son, he bought the post with the gift of a thousand ducats to the order's father provincial. He proudly informed us of this fact. Charming and witty, he follows Epicurea rather than Dominic. Albeit, we appreciated his hospitality.

After stopping overnight at several places, we arrived at the capital with horse and cart. It is built on and around a fabulous lake that is divided into a salty part and a fresh one. In the latter fish abound and the water is good and healthful.

Because of trade and agriculture and gold and silver, México is one of the richest and largest cities in the world. More than twenty ships arrive yearly at the port of Veracruz from Spain. In Puerto Rico, a year easily elapses before just one appears. South from here is commerce with Perú. To the West at Acapulco come ships and goods from Japan, China and the Philippines.

Yesterday we supped with my brother, Antonio Blas, now a distinguished Dominican theologian at the University. World-famed and beautiful in gardens, grounds and architecture, it is a delight.

With reason, Antonio has no wish to go elsewhere. This resembles paradise on earth. The library is immense.

The plaza mercado is big, rich and varied. Everything is offered in the covered stalls. Fine silks. Porcelain. Wood carvings. Medicinal herbs from here and the Orient. All manner of cups and plates and jewelry in gold, silver, copper and bronze. It seems a world market, surely grander than anything in the Old World.

We have been staying at the home of Andrés's cousin, Gonzalo. He has a fine, stout house on Calle San Agustín, which is where most of the silk merchants live. He is a good host, generous to his guests.

Two days ago, he took us to a park-like area called Alameda. It is the fashion here for all the gallants to go there on horseback or carriage each day at about four in the afternoon. Then the people of fashion begin arriving in their fancy carriages. At least 2,000 carriages turn out, from this city of 100,000 homes. The ladies are usually accompanied by their black slaves. Braids and hairpieces are woven with gold and silver. And the men dress sumptuously, too, and go about with a train of slaves behind them. Flirtations and open love affairs seem to intertwine in a bewildering, complicated fashion. Angered by supposed slights and jealousies, the men are always on the verge of swordplay. Each day there's some skirmish over a love match.

Last night Andrés and his cousin had an argument. This wealth, says my husband, is at the cost of enslaving Indians whose home this is. What went before, we may attribute to our ancestors. But what happens now is on our conscience. Of course, I have observed nothing myself – though I have read much by de las Casas and am persuaded by his and Andrés's reasoning. The cousins made peace and decided wisely not to discuss the subject further.

December, 1590
Chiapas

Now we are at Chiapas, where my husband once lived and still owns land and cattle. This, too, is a rich and splendid place, where we will stay a few days before going on to the nearby Indian settlement to meet his children and their mother. Andrés bought me a lovely new frock with material made in China. I put it on for Sunday Mass at the cathedral, and hoped I would not be overdressed.

I could hardly believe my eyes. People looked ready to dance at a formal ball, not to pray. The slaves were as gorgeously attired as their owners, with elaborate dresses in brilliant colors and original designs. All the women carried lacy fans and wore beautiful silk mantillas.

The celebration of Mass was a pagan spectacle. When the priest began to say his sermon, the slaves all got up and left. Back and forth, in and out they went, bringing chocolate to their mistresses. In turn, the ladies laughed and chatted throughout until the poor priest stuttered and then gave up.

This place of Chiapas is infamous in several ways. First was when Bartolomé de las Casas was bishop in 1544. He told his new flock that absolution in the sacrament of Confession depended upon their treatment of the Indian. The Spaniard and *Criollo* were told to free all personal slaves and make restitution for all goods taken from the native. The upshot was rebellion. The flock literally drove the pastor out. Back in Spain, he continued to argue the same message.

But Chiapas remained unrepentant. They must have gained a great deal of confidence in their perversity. Later on, a new bishop of Chiapas tried to reform the way Mass was being attended. He scolded the people, saying they must be quiet during his sermons and chocolate could no longer be served. Anyone who dared to disobey would be excommunicated.

The bishop and the congregation fought, but this cleric didn't return to Spain. He died mysteriously and his body bloated terribly. Tongues wag that poison was put in his chocolate because of his strictness, giving rise to the saying, "Beware the chocolate of Chiapas."

The present bishop obviously does not dare exercise his authority in this vainglorious crowd. He prefers to avoid chocolate.

\*\*\*

At last the day arrived. For the last years I'd been both fearful and curious to meet Andrés's sons and their mother, María Isabel.

As we rode towards the settlement, some leagues from the city, Andrés squeezed my hand. "Please don't be frightened," he said. "This all happened before you married me. Though I still love them, it's as though from another life. I hope you will like each other."

The settlement of some 4,000 families is called Villa Chiapas. Its beauty took away my breath. Built on the banks of a fresh, quickly-running river, the Villa is prosperous and well laid out, with pleasant gardens and buildings. In the center is a well-built convent and church, harmonious in design and in better condition than our cathedral at home. Two busy sugarmills grind the cane, one belonging to the Dominicans. The other belongs to the Indians. Together with 200 black slaves, they produce sugar to sell throughout the whole region. They raise excellent horses which are prized throughout México. They farm wheat and other grain, especially corn.

The first to plant wheat here in the New World was Juan Garrido, a black African prince who first came to Puerto Rico as a conquistador with Ponce de León. After conquering the Aztecs, Garrido sowed the first seeds of wheat in México.

As we rode through this place, I could not help but marvel. Andrés spoke to me about the entertainments here. He said in horseracing, art, music, and dancing the Indians excel the Spaniard. Even their theater of Spanish and Indian works is outstanding. "You should see the way they do *Fuenteovejuna* or *Lazarillo de Tormes*! Depending on the audience, the actors will do the play in Spanish or their native tongue. And wait until tomorrow, an important feast day. GUADALUPE! You have never seen such a superb festival, visually and spiritually. Just wait. I'll say no more."

At last he pulled the carriage to a halt, in front of a two-story straw and wooden house. It is gracious in design, and has a bath house in the patio. Andrés says they bathe in hot water at the slightest pretext, thinking it helps them repel disease. I wonder if there's anything to it.

We stepped down from the carriage and waited in front of the house. Then a striking looking woman emerged. María Isabel. She is of medium height, well-formed, with light copper skin and long, black braided hair that has silver ornaments. The expression on her face was tranquil and dignified, as would befit a queen.

Her fine wool dress was elaborately embroidered and gathered at the waist by a belt of silver. I was moved to a mixture of conflicting emotion: sadness, envy, delight, respect.

We all more or less bowed to each other, and then she lifted her hand. Two youngsters shot out of the house, leaping onto their father like two young panthers. They were dark and beautiful like their mother, though with the big bones of their father.

María Isabel beckoned us to follow her to the patio behind the house. A servant brought us hot chocolate and delicious corn cakes. I spoke little, merely listened to the conversation about the children and details of the transaction that Andrés was arranging. Since he'd written earlier, there were no surprises.

Her stoic expression was common among the Indians, I knew, so her lack of smiling was not upsetting. She looked directly at me for the first time and spoke, "You will be a good wife for Andrés in the world of the Spaniard. I am pleased."

Then she turned back to Andrés as their conversation continued. His two young sons stood next to him the whole time, and he had his arms around them. I felt eyes on me, and looked around. On the second floor of the house, someone pulled away from the window. Her parents, I imagined, since I knew they lived together.

I began listening to the mother discussing her children. "They read and write very well. They could become scholars or poets if they wish. Like their idol el Inca Garcilaso de la Vega, who was warrior next to the prince of Spain and now is the greatest poet of the realm, living in Andalucía. Like them, he is *mestizo* of noble birth." She gazed intently at Andrés, waiting.

He spoke in measured tones, emphasizing his words so the boys would give them importance. "Yes, he is a man of great honor and virtue. As our sons are, he is an *hidalgo*, high-born from both Spain and Indian families. And they, too, will bring great respect to both sides."

Satisfied and nodding in agreement, she continued. "Your sons also play the viola as I do, and they sing like nightingales. You will hear tomorrow at Mass."

"No," said Andrés, "sing for us now. Please."

The boys looked at their mother, who barely moved her head in accord. The elder of the two, Federico, motioned to his brother to join him. Standing next to each other, they began to sing a lovely and timeless *villancico*. We all smiled fulsomely and hoped for more. Then a marvelous song by Monteverdi, sweet and lofting as angels. My heart felt like breaking with the joy of the music. It was a most extraordinary moment, and I remember nothing further of the meeting. It was though a trance had occurred.

The next day, though, was also as marvelous as María Isabel had promised. We arrived early to be sure we could all sit together. An accomplished Indian organist played wonderful music based on but not quite like Gregorian chant as we waited for the church to fill up. Then trumpets announced the procession of the celebrants. The priest and acolytes walked down the main aisle, wearing brocaded vestments interwoven with Indian and Spanish symbols. The carved wooden and gold high altar blazed with beeswax candles. At the side was a splendid chapel to Our Lady of Guadalupe to honor the Virgin Mary who had appeared to Juan Diego of Tolpetlac, a Mexican Indian, at the foot of Tepeyac in 1531.

A choir of perhaps a hundred children burst into the Kyrie. The whole church joined the sung liturgy. I could not believe the beauty of it.

For the recessional, the choir sang a modern polyphonic Italian hymn that would have inspired the Pope himself. To return from this to Puerto Rico would be leaving Spanish Indian civilization for a bucolic Spanish Caribbean rusticity. Perhaps I could help sponsor a better-trained choir than the one that now sang at the cathedral...Until one had heard something like this, it wasn't possible to appreciate what human voice and spirit could attain.

Just moments later, when all the congregation had filed out, another extraordinary act began on the church steps. A dance group of young men and women portrayed acts from the life of Christ, singing in their Indian tongue and accompanied with native flute and drum.

They were dressed in wonderful costumes with plumes and ribbons, and moved in rare harmony. The grace and beauty of their dance and song perfectly complemented the excellence of the European music in church. Truly, such extraordinary beauty in song and movement I could never have dreamed. This day will forever haunt my spirit.

As Andrés finished the legal arrangements during the next days, I wandered about the Villa. His sons were so learned for their age that I decided to use them as models for the education of our own children. They were already skilled in Latin, Spanish, their native tongue, mathematics and music. And, wonderfully, they had a sense of humor. They were fun, not like some of the shriveled young scholars we see at home. They took us to an exciting canoe race on the river that ran through the village, to a bullfight which was better than anything I'd seen at home, to an artisans' studio. We admired carvings and musical instruments and household articles, all crafted here. At the printing press, I was shown translations of Ovid and Petrarch that had been translated by *mestizos* to the Indian tongue. I felt as though I'd somehow encountered More's Utopia. If he had visited here, he would have reshaped his book to reflect this powerful aesthetic sense that Christian Indian and Spanish created. Would such beauty and excellence inspire the future? Would Europe and the Indies learn from this?

At last the notary and priest and legal guardians and María Isabel and Andrés sorted out the children's trust. With all in order, it came time to say farewell.

This time Andrés hugged María Isabel, who remained apparently unmoved. The sons were admonished to be good and brave and care for their mother. They agreed, of course. He said, "Someday we will return, I hope. But when you are big, perhaps you can visit us in Puerto Rico."

I saw María Isabel face express rejection of that last comment. Even should they reach the stature of el Inca, she would not want them to leave México. Only here would they truly belong.

We left, she and I staring at each other with a sense of understanding and strangeness. *Adiós, adiós.*

I could not help but puzzle on Andrés. If he were capable of leaving such grace and achievement, what then might lie ahead? Would he also tire of me?

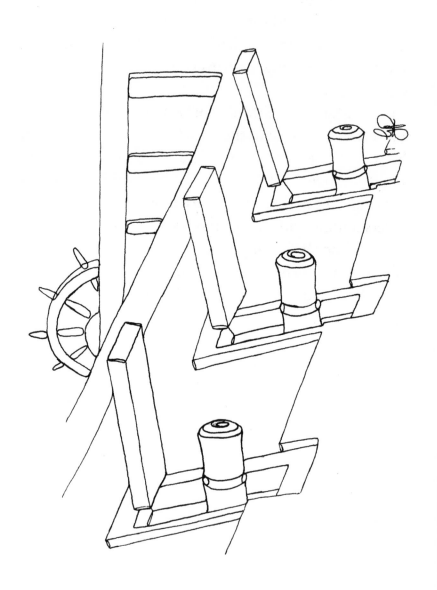

## Chapter Nine

E ven such a great writer of profound mind such as Inca Garcilaso de la Vega, though son of Inca princess and Spanish conquistador, saw himself apart in the world. He said in an introduction to his accomplished work, "I ask that you receive this in the same spirit that I present it, and the fault which it has you will pardon me because I am Indian, and therefore for being barbarous and not taught in science nor math...." After seeing Chiapas and realizing El Inca's brilliance, I must conclude that he was capable of great irony.

February, 1591
Puerto Rico

On the way back to Puerto Rico Andrés regaled me with real tales and legends from this part of the world. Coming on the coattails of Villa Chiapas and México, such a mixture of the phantasmagoric and harsh reality, all told under the vast starry sky of the Caribbean Sea: all this has transformed the way I see life. Nothing will be the same. Ever. It is as though another dimension has unfolded in the material world. Dreams and remembrances vibrate with the same force as the senses, delicately hovering in the shadows to give shape to what is real and true. My existence in Puerto Rico is the richer for it, and I no longer have to yearn to see another world. It is part of me now.

How good to see my son Esteban! At first, he hardly remembered his parents, but within days we are once again at ease.

Again, I am pregnant, I hope the second of many to come.

I am growing to know my husband. He is a good man, as I'd hoped. But he is cursed by eternal restlessness. He tires of routine. He will stare it seems for hours at the horizon on the sea's edge. Only duty keeps him from going off to Perú or the Pacific Ocean beyond. I cannot but remember his abandonment of his family in Chiapas. Though I love him dearly and most humanly, my true happiness cannot rest on his.

And yet I understand him, for I too am prey to another kind of restlessness. More than ever, I must seek beyond the apparent. Books help. Thought and prayer. And of course, tending to my child. And even swimming in the ocean and walking through the land in Bayamón and San Germán, feasting the eye on lush green growth. But I must keep pursuing ideas and probe the meaning of things. Do others on this island suffer this anxiety to know and feel? The life here does not facilitate exchange of such thoughts. So, I communicate and treat as my dearest friends, one-sidedly of course, such as Sor Juana Inés de la Cruz and Erasmus of Rotterdam.

Erasmus expresses himself so clearly, with grace and simplicity. His thoughts reflect my own aspirations. Of Christ's philosophy, for example, he says it centers his life as "it is a synthesis of theology and spirituality, made of knowledge and love, enriched by meditation, prayer and sacrifice, crowned with union with God...it is not only intellectual for it's accessible to the most humble...it makes God understandable, as we ask for humility, fraternity, knowledge and life."

Yet Erasmus is not a stoic. He treasures good wine and conversation and things of beauty as well. He criticizes pompous churchmen.

He disapproves of self-serving platitudes. Life is too full, too rich, too fleeting, not to try to embrace it whole. God give me time and health and opportunity to enjoy it!

Late November, 1595
San Juan
At last the attack, so long feared. Twenty-four armed ships led by Francis Drake have appeared off the coast. Though our island is so poor, in the depths of La Fortaleza lie two million ducats worth of gold and silver. The treasure was left for keeping by a damaged flagship en route to Spain, and word got to the English.

Drake is a cunning devil. But thank God that our Governor Pedro Suárez is a match for the English dragon.

He ordered two ships sunk in the bay's only entry channel to effectively keep out the enemy's ships. Within the bay waited five Spanish frigates to fire on smaller vessels.

Families and slaves sought refuge in the country. Our three children, four servants and I left San Juan for the Rio Bayamón *estancia*, while Andrés joined the nobles' militia to protect the city walls. Meanwhile reinforcements have streamed into San Juan from the island. El Morro and the outlying fortifications have seventy cannon and 1,550 men.

On November 22, the English ships were positioned on the other side of the bay's mouth, next to Caleta de Cabrón and El Morillo. Cannon shot was exchanged between them and the fort and a cannon ball shattered Drake's very dining table where he sat with John Hawkins. Hawkins died in the act, and Drake quickly moved the ship out of range.

For one day nothing happened.

Then at ten o'clock at night, Drake's men launched an attack of burning arrows at our frigates in the bay. At the same time the English stormed our ships and fierce fighting erupted. For an hour it continued, until the English fell back. The next day, Drake's fleet was gone. Even so, they went on to burn a sugarmill and sack the town of Aguada. They let loose five Spanish captured in the San Juan Bay, and sailed off to seek an easier prize.

We returned to the city today to massive huzzahs. Everyone crowded in front of the cathedral, singing a Mass of thanksgiving. Then thousands of us – the whole town and more filled the streets in procession, mightily singing the "Te Deum" and following the bishop and the priests and the *hermandades* and every cross and saint from the church and monastery hoisted above. One stanza would end and another end, floating like a wave of sound through the jubilant hodgepodge. Not even the notes in Villa Chiapas sounded so sweet!

Then, riding on their groomed and prancing horses, came the governor and the cavalry of *hidalgos*, including Andrés and Father. The jingling of the bells fixed on the saddles made nice counterpoint to the rhythmic clop of the hooves on the packed earthen streets.

We pray no evil will follow.

The new governor, Antonio Mosquera, has not been so bad as some. Sent a year after Drake's attack, he brought money, slaves and soldiers to finish building El Morro. He found a militia that's debilitated morally and physically. To placate some of the pent-up resentments, he has listened to the people complain of past and present abuses. In truth, the list is long. Opportunists lie and insinuate cunningly, jostling to sit next the seat of power. Mosquera does not know whom to believe. Meanwhile, the new slaves and soldiers easily fall to tropical disease and fever.

Andrés is sick of it all. And I, surely. I pray we may go to his family lands in San Germán. There we can live on cattle and clandestine trade, as does everyone there. They have, I think, a freer life than we in San Juan, where with so little, we pretend so much. I hope Father will join us if we go. Though more vulnerable to attack from the sea, San Germán itself would be less harsh a life.

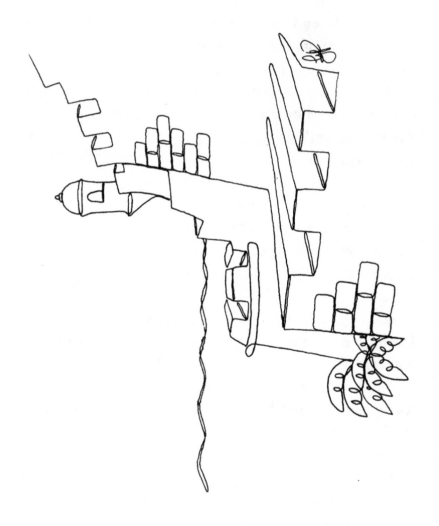

# Chapter Ten

June 18, 1598 San Juan

What cruel jokes does life play! The English hold us captive. Andrés is either dead or captive. My father is dead. The Count of Cumberland, George Clifford, with twenty ships and 1,000 troops took us by surprise. Attacking from the land side, Cangrejos, they came towards a weakly defended flank. At first repulsed from trying to cross the little wooden bridge before the fort at Caño San Antonio, they then regrouped and landed boats next to Escambrón, behind our soldiers. Clifford fell into the water in San Antonio, with all his armor. What a pity they fished him out in time!

Governor Mosquera and some troops, including my father and husband on horseback, arrived to do battle. But faced with a superior force, most of our soldiers deserted. Father was hit in the head with a musket ball and killed instantly. He died as he had lived, honorably and without fanfare. He was a good man, through and through. Andrés was last seen surrounded, fighting with his sword. I must be prepared for his death.

The governor and the men remaining fell back to El Morro, where they are now barricaded, refusing to surrender.

The city is almost deserted, except for a few unhappy souls. We are here because the children took fever and could not be moved. A few hours ago, the English entered the houses. We are fortunate that ours attracted their chaplain, John Layfield. I have hopes that as a man of God, even a heretical one, he will help defend us from the soldiers' brutality. Perhaps the children's fever will also frighten them away.

It's the first time I've heard their language. English sounds so strange and harsh. Guttural and ugly. Knowing their hate for Spain and the Church makes my blood run cold.

June 25, 1598
San Juan

The English chaplain and I communicate with a sort of combination of hand language, Latin and Spanish. He tells me that an English soldier was hanged in the Plaza de las Verduras for raping the wife of a Spaniard. She is a friend of mine, the poor woman! She will be happy to hear of the brute's punishment, well-deserved. Better that they kill off all the beasts, these vile Englishmen! The chaplain tells me that Clifford has given strict orders against attacking civilians, looting and vandalizing the churches.

The hanging will reinforce the message. But men at war become true savages. How long will this go on? Will these English people stay forever and destroy our lives utterly?

June 30, 1598
San Juan

Mosquera has given up the fort, having run through provisions. None of us has food to speak of. The epidemic rages, but Esteban and María Mercedes are slowly recovering. Thank God I still have my strength. The English have shipped away Mosquera and many of his officials, I know not where.

Still no news of Andrés.

The English have raised their flag. But when they foray into the countryside, our *campesinos* and deserters shoot from cover. Now the enemy has begun to set fires in the countryside. Two mills in Loíza were torched. I hope they don't reach ours in Bayamón, which, poor as it may be, can sustain me and the children.

The English are falling mightily to the epidemic. If enough get sick enough and hungry enough, perhaps they'll go. I am becoming frightened of the officers billeted next door...The way they look at me...

August 14, 1598
San Juan

The English devils have gone. And not empty-handed. Slaves, pearls, sugar, ginger, church bells, the church organ, sacramental vessels and all the guns and cannon Clifford and his fleet could carry. They sacked the church and many of the houses. Margarita and I had buried the silver in the patio the evening of their cursed arrival, so from us they took little. The threatening soldiers from next door went with their commander, thank God. But behind they left an officer, John Berkley, to hold this poor battered island for the English.

September 5, 1598
San Juan

Berkley and his cohorts have left, driven away by hunger and plague. I can hardly believe the children, Margarita and I survived. And what of my husband?

September 8, 1598
San Juan

Andrés is still weak. But alive. After being run through with a sword and left for dead, he was rescued by a deserter and taken to the hills to join the escaped slaves, the *cimarrones*. One of them, a man named Orlando, nursed him back to health. When the English left, he brought Andrés to the edge of San Juan and left him under a tree with a skin of water. If the *cimarrón* were caught, he would be horribly whipped and tortured to death. What a grave risk he took! Orlando will always be in our family prayers. And who knows? perhaps someday we may repay him...

Our home, our spirits, our family have been ravished. Now to the mill on the Río Bayamón, to rest and build up our strength with good food. And then, on to San Germán. To begin our lives again.

I am sure I feel the stirring of new life in me. Another child. It is surely a sign from God of good things to come. A renewal of life in the aftermath of death and destruction. *Deo gratias.*

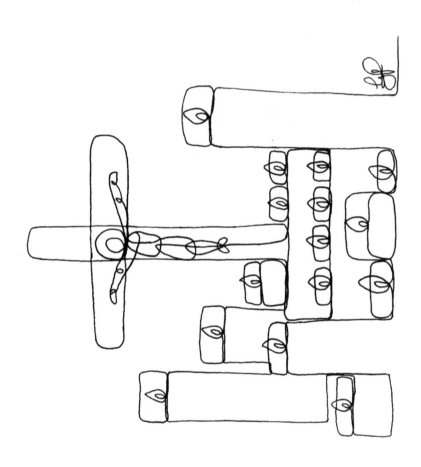

## Chapter Eleven

October 1650
San Juan

Looking through this old journal and seeing the faded script on dry, crackling pages plunges me into the past. I recall my own mother, near her untimely death, speaking of her girlhood in the famed walled city of Ávila. How she felt like the same child who had run after the family's herd of sheep as the blustery snow whipped off the rock-spotted mountain. The same child who pled with her dearest friend Teresa if she, too, could not accompany her and her brother Rodrigo, as they were going off to convert the Moors. At the time none of them were over nine years old. And later on, as a young woman at the Augustinian convent where she studied until the marriage with my father was arranged by her parents, and she lived a while in Salamanca. Mother's memories became mine.

As one gets older, the body weakens. Eyes need more light to read by. One can no longer mount a horse in one easy leap. Even walking demands a certain concentration, as dimming vision must search out obstacles on a rocky path. I regard my own image in the looking glass today with what I hope is my accustomed honesty. My finger traces the fine wrinkles that spread out from my eyes like tendrils of an uprooted fern. Just as trees show their longevity by rings in their trunk, so faces display their age in lines.

My hair is streaked with grey but still lustrous, thanks to the coconut water I wash it in. I wear it in a long braid, which then is pinned to the back of my head. Not so fashionable perhaps, but neat. I still walk upright and with a sure though slower step.

If I've slept well, I rise early for Mass at the Carmelite convent, where I can then join my granddaughter for a light breakfast. I sew a bit in the morning – mending, really, because I never did become adept at decorative embroidery – and read for a couple of hours and edit this journal.

Ana (whose husband, thanks be to God and our own machinations, ran off to Perú many years ago) and I often have a light lunch together. We give reading classes to her maid and some girls in the neighborhood, and then chat about everything from poetry, especially that of México's Sor Juana de la Cruz which we set to music, to grandchildren. From how the fruit trees are doing to a little gossip about the newest government officials. Frequently we play the *laúd* and sing old melodies from Andalucía or newer ones that we make up.

Perhaps twice a week, my spiritual director calls for *merienda* – a cake and a glass of sherry – and we discuss new books as well as the state of my soul. Almost each evening I stroll around the plaza, where I can greet the new and old faces of our little community. And at least once a week, I head for a more vigorous walk, up to the grounds approaching El Morro Fortress, where I can feel the wind come off the sea, and glory in the vastness and beauty of God's universe.

Always, my maidservant Carmen María, (granddaughter of Tomás, who bought his freedom so many years ago) walks with me. My dear Margarita died years ago of a fever. She became like my sister, and is always in my prayers. I want everyone in my household to appreciate learning, so have taught them all at least their basic letters. Carmen María has a lovely voice and a good mind, so each night she reads to me for an hour. My favorite readings are *Mi vida* by Teresa de Ávila, *Don Quijote de la mancha* by Miguel de Cervantes Saavedra. Oftentimes, we chant the psalms together.

Of the six children I bore Andrés, only two still live. Of those who died, two perished when very young, another was a Jesuit martyred in Japan, and the fourth died at sea in a storm. Of the two who remain, María Mercedes is now a Benedictine prioress in México, where she met my favorite poet, Sor Juana de la Cruz. The other is Esteban, a great landowner and rancher in San Germán, where he sired a large family, not all within wedlock. He has six legitimate and four other legally acknowledged children (from different women, born before he married his wife, to whom I trust he is faithful). Only three of his children are here, while the other half have scattered around the world. Esteban, whom I remember as such a loving, bright and stubborn child, is now the *cacique* or chief of the region. I am told he is a good leader. But would anyone speak badly of him to an old mother? He is always in my prayers.

The youngest is in San Germán, while two are in San Juan. One, Victoria, is a nun at the new Carmelite convent and the other, Raúl, is a captain at El Morro, hoping for a transfer to Cartagena or México. Most of the grandchildren live outside Puerto Rico: in México, a Dominican priest who teaches at the University, thus following the steps of my brother Antonio Blas; a Benedictine nun where her aunt (my daughter) is prioress; another who is married to a high government official; two grandsons in Santo Domingo, both military officers and ranch owners. The youngest is a Jesuit priest in the Philippines, while the oldest is a ship's captain in the Orient. I wonder if he ever saw dear Francisco Javier, my brother.

And, of course, Andrés. Many years ago – it seems a century – he died of wounds suffered while beating off French corsairs from our *estancia* in San Germán. For three months he lingered in great pain, and then his spirit left. To remember still shakes me, and I try not to think upon it.

It is said that in Spain a third of the population is monk, priest, lay brother, oblate or nun. My family reflects that.

But to return to my own condition. The process of ageing is not so much a blow to one's vanity, though surely that enters the picture. I've always known my youthful beauty was but a fleeting gift from God, to be appreciated but not overly treasured. No, in physical appearance, I am content to be neat and simply well-dressed. The austerity of classical Spanish dress now appeals to me. It is a style that is dignified for the old, just as it is too stark for the young.

No, the deepest fear of an ageing body is anticipating the end. The realization that death awaits.

On one hand my faith in God and our Holy Catholic Church give me succor. In a strange way, though not actually welcoming death, I look forward to it with hope and even curiosity. What a paradox!

Yet who can deny the fear and doubt that lie below the surface of the firmest faith? If all is but oblivion? Or only a seamless nirvana, as those of the Orient believe? Or worse, reincarnation into another creature – how I should hate to be a toad!

I am not even supposed to be aware that such beliefs exist, since the Crown has always limited the books coming to the island. Church officials, especially the Torquemadas of the Inquisition, are consumed with worry.

Books open the mind.

The Church fears that new converts among the Indians and Africans, and even the older, slipsliding Spanish Christians too, would be corrupted by too much learning. Such holy and literate men as Luis de León, the prime interpreter of Teresa of Ávila, have been tormented by the Inquisitors. Most Inquisitors are to be feared and not trusted.

But since we lived so long in San Germán, we eventually had relatively easy access to books from the French corsairs in the clandestine trade that everyone on the southwest coast uses (even the governors and bishops!) So it was that I read many officially forbidden books and learned what was going on in the world.

You, dear reader – likely my descendant – please do not be scandalized by my behavior. Later on, I secretly discussed many of these books with a Dominican priest who had previously read them for his work with the Inquisition. Regulations and laws are often but tools for manipulation in the hands of the cognoscenti. It is especially common in America, where the Spanish-born brandish Spanish law to the detriment of the *criollo* and *mestizo* and *mulato*.

My advice to you on this matter then is: read and study much, even while asking the Holy Spirit for guidance. It is best if you can choose as your spiritual director a holy priest who is also learned and open in mind. I realize that such people are difficult to find in Puerto Rico, and even in Spain. On the other hand, if Spain could give the world such brave spirits as Teresa de Ávila, Juan de la Cruz, Luis de León, and Bartolomé de las Casas – all who defied established authority in the pursuit of the good and the true– then, surely, there is hope that you too may find a noble soul to guide you.

If you prize the world of the intellect, be thankful.

God has given you that special gift, and it should be used. I surely do not advocate promiscuous reading, which can be just as bad for one's spirit as promiscuous friendships. But just as you must be open rather than closed to the good in human encounters – even among those whom society judges unworthy – so you must be open in intellect and spirit, to seek the good and the true. For the love of Christ for us is boundless and relentless. Be honest and fearless in this world of deceit. Beware of those who are too ambitious, be they churchmen, family or friends. Remember: "Nada te turbe."

If you, reader and descendant, should dislike my words, I beg you not to burn or hide this journal from our family. Instead, in loyalty to your blood, give it in safekeeping to him or her who would find some understanding of my thoughts. *Pax.*

## LET NOTHING DISTURB YOU
### *NADA TE TURBE*
-*Santa Teresa de Jesús*


Let nothing disturb you
Let nothing frighten you.
All passes.
God does not move;
Patience
Conquers all: Who has God
Lacks nothing.
God alone suffices.

*Nada te turbe,*
*Nada te espante,*
*Todo se pasa.*
*Dios no se muda;*
*La paciencia*
*Todo lo alcanza; Quien a Dios tiene*
*Nada le falta,*
*Solo Dios basta.*

Lift your thought,
Let it rise to heaven.
Nothing should upset you,
Let nothing disturb you.
*Eleva el pensamiento,*
*Al cielo sube,*
*Por nada te acongojes,*
*Nada te turbe.*

Follow Jesus Christ
With great pride,
And come what may,
Nothing will frighten you.
*A Jesucristo sigue*
*Con pecho grande,*
*Y venga lo que venga,*
*Nada te espante.*

Do you see the world's glory?
It is but vainglory,
Not at all stable,

All will pass.
*¿Ves la gloria del mundo?*
*es gloria vana,*
*Nada tiene de estable,*
*Todo se pasa.*
Aspire to heaven,
That lasts forever;
Faithful and rich in promise,
God does not move.
*Aspira a lo celeste,*
*Que siempre dura:*
*Fiel y rico en promesas*
*Dios no se muda.*
Love that which merits
Immense goodness:
But there is no real love
Without patience.
*Ámale cual merece*
*Bondad inmensa:*
*Pero no hay amor fino*
*Sin la paciencia.*

Let confidence and faith
Maintain the soul;
Who believes and hopes
Will achieve all.
*Confianza y fe viva*
*Mantenga el alma;*
*Pues quien cree y espera*
*Todo lo alcanza.*

From a pursuing hell
Though you may see it,
You mock its furor
You who have God.
Let enter poverty,
Crosses, humiliation;
With God as your treasure
Nothing is lacking.
*Del infierno acosado*
*Aunque se viere,*
*Burlara sus furores*
*Quien a Dios tiene.*
*Véngale desamparos*
*Cruces, desgracias;*
*Siendo Dios tu tesoro*
*Nada le falta.*
Flee, then, goods of the world;
Flee, such vanities,
Though all is lost,
God alone suffices.
*Id, pues, bienes del mundo;*
*Id, dichas vanas,*
*Aunque todo lo pierda,*
*Sólo Dios basta.*

## FIN

# Sources

The *Chronicles of María Teresa de Villalobos* follows the sweep of the history of Puerto Rico with some exceptions; the years of the following people have been moved around a few decades to accommodate to María Teresa's story: Santa Teresa de Jesús; Sor Juana Inés de la Cruz; Baltasar Gracián; Alonso Ramírez; Thomas Gage; Bartolomé de las Casas.

Among other fifteenth and sixteenth century writers, the following are goldmines of first-hand information of those times: Miguel de Cervantes Saavedra, Juan de Castellanos, Gonzalo Fernández de Oviedo, Lope de Vega, Bartolomé de las Casas, Carlos Sigüenza y Góngora, Sor Juana Inés de la Cruz, Santa Teresa de Ávila, San Juan de la Cruz, Erasmus, Thomas More, Thomas Gage, el Inca Garcilaso de la Vega, Baltasar Gracián, Damián López de Haro, De Torres Vargas. Some of these are quoted in the compilations in nineteenth century Alejandro Tapia y Rivera, *Biblioteca histórica* and twentieth century Eugenio Méndez, *Crónicas de Puerto Rico*.

Twentieth century historians include Salvador Brau, *Historia de Puerto Rico*; María Teresa Babín, *Panorama de la cultura puertorriqueña*; Adolfo de Hostos, *Historia de San Juan, ciudad murada*; Ludwig Pfandl, *Introducción al Siglo de Oro*; Samuel E. Morison's maritime expertise in *The European Discovery of America*; Ricardo E. Alegría, essays about black conquistador Juan Garrido and other historical figures, which I translated for him and that appeared in THE SAN JUAN STAR Sunday Magazine during 1992.

# Acknowledgements

Before all, thank you - posthumously - to all those fascinating writers of the Spanish *siglo de oro* who wrote about Puerto Rico. The rich history of Puerto Rico is practically unknown outside the island. When I discovered it years ago, I felt I was entering another world. Bravo!

Many thanks due to dear friends and assiduous readers of María Teresa de Villalobos's story through the years, since it first appeared in the SAN JUAN STAR Sunday Magazine (now defunct). The Pulitzer-winning STAR editor Andrew Viglucci and Sunday magazine editor Connie Underhill featured much of the story in a monthly series with great display and artwork. The DC Arts and Humanities Council, propelled by Paquita Vivó, invited me to give a talk in Washington about the daily life of a sixteenth century Puerto Rican woman. Institute of Puerto Rican Culture founder Ricardo Alegría greatly encouraged my studies about Puerto Rican history, and we collaborated on several projects, including my classes in English on Puerto Rican history at the Centro de Estudios Avanzados in Old San Juan. Author and friend Shea Megale encouraged me to include a chapter for the Chantilly, Fairfax, Virginia Public Library writers' edition in 2016.

In 2018 Puerto Rico retired director of Casa del Libro and friend María Teresa Arrarás advised me to have the Institute of Puerto Rican Culture print the book. Meanwhile my gifted designer daughter in law Leamir Candamo Pou was raving about the manuscript and saying it must enter the modern world through internet. She has helped so much in the production. Dear friends Donna Sabater, Teresita Bolívar, Anne Chevako and Mariam Guillemard have encouraged my writing. Special thanks to Ken Oliver, Jay Chevako and Gabriela Pérez. My recent three novels, all contemporary and set in various sites including Puerto Rico will soon be published. Of course, always, thanks to my dear husband, Roberto, and our wonderful family!

## Suggested topics for book club discussion

- The place of woman in society
- Changes in thought and everyday life from María Teresa's time to the present
- The importance of Teresa de Ávila in María Teresa's life
- The role of the Church in everyday life at the time
- The role of the Inquisition in Spain and the Colonies
- The richness of Mexico and the poverty of Puerto Rico
- The cultural rivalry between Spain and England
- The reality of slaves and Indians
- Controversies between Church and Crown
- The scope of Spain's global power
- The reflections of poetry on real life

CPSIA information can be obtained
at www.ICGtesting.com
Printed in the USA
LVHW03s1800230818
587902LV00005B/763/P